From Ratchet To Riche$ 3

Patrice Balark

From Ratchet To Riches 3

Copyright © 2019 by Patrice Balark
All rights reserved.
Published in the United States of America.
All rights reserved. No part of this publication may be reproduced, distributed, or transmitted in any form or by any means, including photocopying, recording, or other electronic or mechanical methods, without the prior written permission of the publisher, except in the case of brief quotations embodied in critical reviews and certain other noncommercial uses permitted by copyright law. For permission requests, please contact: www.authortwylat.com.
This is a work of fiction. Names, characters, places, and incidents either are the products of the author's imagination or are used fictitiously. Any resemblance of actual persons, living or dead, businesses, companies, events, or locales is entirely coincidental. The publisher does not have any control and does not assume any responsibility for author or third-party websites or their content.

Published by Twyla T. Presents, LLC.

Last Time In, From Ratchet to Riche$

"Wait Capone, tell me what happened again from the top please!" Diamond laughed into the phone as Capone hit the expressway and blunt.

"Man look…. I'm not finna tell the story again Diamond, especially when you think the shit funny." He barked, releasing the smoke from his mouth.

"I'm sorry bro. I just can't believe Pip thought she was gon' shade my girl and get away with it. I can't wait to talk to Mecca." Diamond continued laughing from the other end as she had been doing the whole conversation.

"Wait. You talked to Mecca? She ain't answering my calls." He replied, feeling his anger grow because he despised being ignored.

"Yeah…. Well briefly anyway. She was leaving Kool's crib. Matter fact, she said she'll call me back cuz she was getting on the elevator." Diamond remembered.

"Aight bet. She at the crib huh?" Capone said aloud, not particular to Diamond but just in general.

"Imma call you when I leave her crib."

"CAPONE, DON'T POP UP ON THAT GIRL! WHAT IF HER NIGGA THERE?!" Diamond yelled into the phone, but her screams didn't faze Capone.

"Then I'll kill him if he gets out his body." He warned, ending the call in his big sister's ear.

Doing as promised, Capone headed to the condo, honestly not caring if buddy was there or not. He had to talk to Mecca and planned on doing it, one way or another.

"What up Ava?" Capone said, answering his ringing phone as he pulled in front of the condo.

"Where you at?" her voice blared through the speakers.

"Taking care of some business. What up?" he asked again, hoping there was a reason for the call.

"Well, I was sitting here thinking and the way you handled the situation yesterday with that lil bitch…

"MECCA…" he corrected her.

"Like I said, I was sitting here thinking and I don't like the way you handled the situation. For you to say that y'all friends and nothing never happened between y'all, y'all sure do seem a little funny acting." She continued with an attitude.

"Like I explained yesterday baby, it ain't shit between me and Mecca. I respect shorty and the shit she's done for me."

"What the fuck did she do for you?" she quickly snapped.

"She looked out for me when I had a little work on me, and she took a gun charge for me Ava. Anything else?"

Capone felt being truthful with Pip was the best thing to do, especially since he truly didn't have anything to hide.

"A GUN CHARGE? YOU DOING ALL THIS FOR A FUCKN HOODRAT?" she laughed sinisterly into the phone, causing Capone to turn down the volume.

"Seriously though Capone, why didn't you tell me any of this?" she continued, calming down a little.

"Because there wasn't shit to tell, but Imma call you back." He replied, ending the call in her face.

Stepping out the car, Capone checked his surroundings before proceeding forward in the building.

"Mr. Brown. How's it going?" Alex the office manager spoke as he headed towards the elevators.

"Alex, my main man. What's up with your Packers this year, my manz?" Capone laughed, pressing the button.

"Ohhhhh… better than ya Bears my friend." Alex replied in a heavy Indian accent.

Capone stood in the elevator alone, trying to figure out why he was popping up on a woman that was *not* his woman. He peeped Mecca kissing dude back at the restaurant, and it honestly made him lose it. Unknowingly, he began taking his anger out on Pip. She was already working his nerves and Mecca only added fuel to the fire.

Knocking at the door twice, Capone checked his waist, making sure his pistol was ready in case that nigga Kool was ready. Fighting over bitches was never his thing, but if homie wanted to act stupid, Capone was with the shits.

"What the fuck are you doing here?" Mecca yanked the door open and asked before walking away.

Staring at her ass in the boy shorts she wore, Capone felt his dick rising as he slowly closed the door, following behind her.

"Aye look, I ain't come over here to argue. I wanna talk to you." Capone said calmly, taking a seat on one of the bar stools in the kitchen.

"Listen…. I don't wanna argue either, but I do feel like there is a conversation that needs to be held." She replied, taking a seat on the stool next to him.

Spinning around, Capone faced the side of Mecca's face. Grabbing her chair, he twisted her around, forcing her to look him in the eyes.

"I really appreciate all you've done Capone, but I've been thinking about moving out and getting a job….."

"Moving out? A job for what? I told you I got you and I mean that shit." He grabbed her hand and stated.

Capone watched Mecca's eyes shift from his hands to his eyes. He didn't care if he was overstepping his boundaries, he didn't want Mecca to leave.

"Yes, with me getting serious with Kool…"

"You getting serious with that nigga?" He cut her off and asked, feeling some type of way.

"I mean, yeah Capone. Ain't that's how relationships usually work? I don't get it though. You damn near walking down the aisle, worrying about what I got going on." She replied truthfully.

"Mannnnn…. It's hard to explain." He laughed it off, standing to his feet, stretching.

After almost cracking every bone in his body, Capone glanced at Mecca, who was sitting in the same spot, staring at an empty space on the floor.

"What you thinking about?" he asked, grabbing her chin, lifting her head.

Mecca and Capone locked eyes before she started smiling. It was crazy how beautiful she was and her growth was scary. The *woman* that sat in front of him now was not the same *girl* he met six months ago.

"You hungry?" she asked, catching him off guard, breaking eye contact.

"Ummmm…. Nah…." He stepped back and said, allowing Mecca room to move.

"A lie. Yo stomach growling. I got you though cuz yo bitch don't look like she can cook anyway." Mecca shaded, walking towards the refrigerator.

Capone watched as she placed bacon, sausage, eggs, milk, and butter on the countertop. Smiling slightly, he watched as she moved about the kitchen like she was raised there. Constantly trying to adjust his dick in his sweats, Capone thought about placing Mecca on top of the counter and eating her pussy.

"Cheese in yo eggs and grits?" she turned to him and said from her spot at the stove.

Shaking his head up and down, Capone continued to watch lil Mecca move like a grown woman.

"So how's school?" he asked, grabbing a water out the fridge, returning back to his stool.

"That shit so easy. I can pass those classes in my sleep." She boasted.

"Aw word. What's your major again?" he quizzed.

"Business and all my classes are already advanced so I'm just cruising through." She continued bragging, turning Capone on even more.

Shaking his head up and down, Capone mentally noted everything Mecca was saying. She had a certain type of drive about her that most young girls her age did not have.

"What you plan on doing with that degree?" he leaned on the counter and asked, watching her bend over checking on the biscuits that was in the oven.

"I wanna own several businesses throughout the hood. Look at our neighborhood and shit. Everything is owned by these Arabs and they rude as fuck, treat us like shit when we enter their establishment." She rambled on as she made their plates.

After pilling the food on, she filled two wine glasses with orange juice before sliding everything over to him.

"This look good." He speculated, looking at the feast she had prepared in such little time.

"It tastes better. Just eat."

Capone caught Mecca looking at him out the side of her eye as she said that last comment. If he knew any better, he would think she was flirting with him, but seeing how Mecca didn't move like that, he let it go.

Feeding his face, Capone was impressed at how delicious the food was. He never took her as the type to cook since their generation was fascinated with fast food.

"Aye…. What would be the first…… business you open up in the …… hood?" Capone asked through smacks.

Without thinking, Mecca quickly answered his question.

"A Beauty Supply." She stated, reaching across the counter, grabbing her phone.

"Everything cool?" Capone questioned, noticing a distressed look on Mecca's face as she checked her phone.

"Ummm yeah. Everything cool. I just haven't talked to my sister in about day then the killer part it, she ain't even come home last night. That's not like her." Mecca explained, picking up Capone's empty plate and taking it to the sink.

"She not answering her phone?"

"Nope. It's going to voicemail like its dead or something."

"Damn, wanna ride through the city looking for her? Maybe stop at some of her homies' house to see if they seen her." Capone suggested, standing to his feet, ready to move on Mecca's call.

"Nah, maybe later." She sighed from the sink where she began making dish water.

Slowly walking towards her, Capone stood behind Mecca as she fumbled with the dishes in the sink.

"Oh, I'm sorry. Am I in your way or something?" she turned around, colliding into him and laughing.

Staring into her eyes, Capone tried to think of an excuse as to why he was invading her personal space; too bad for him, he couldn't think of anything to say.

"Don't she work or sum? You tried calling her job?" he mentioned, stepping back and changing the subject.

"Tuh!" she huffed, wiping her wet hands off on a napkin.

"Danielle is so secretive, getting simple information out of her is like pulling teeth. I ain't got no number." She continued.

Capone had only been around Mecca's sister Danielle a handful of times. She didn't come off as the sneaky type, but then again, he didn't know the girl.

"Go look in her room, it gotta be a check stub or something laying around with her employer information on there." He suggested again, trying his best to help Mecca out.

"You know what? You right. I'll be back."

Capone watched Mecca's ass bounce away as she headed towards the back of the condo where the bedrooms were located. Heading over to the couch, Capone grabbed the remote and cut the 72-inch flat screen on before flopping down on the couch.

Memories of when he first moved into the place at the tender age of eighteen invaded his mind. Shaking his head at the amount of pussy he got in that crib, Capone was starting to miss the days when was able to run around freely.

"This all I found… a business card."

Hearing Mecca's voice snapped Capone out of his trance. Looking up, she stood in front of him and reached out her hand, handing him the card. Taking it from her, Capone flipped it over. The contents on the other side of the white and lavender small card almost gave him a heart attack.

"Aye. Where you get this from?" he quizzed, reading over Pip's contact information.

"Out her drawer. Why, what's wrong?"

The sound of Capone's phone ringing stopped him from replying. Grabbing the device out of his pocket, he unlocked it before reading the message that was on screen.

"CAPONE! What's wrong?" he heard Mecca yell out while he tried piecing everything together.

"This--- this card?" He said, holding it in the air while staring at the picture message sent to him.

"Okaayyyy, what about it?" Mecca probed.

"Danielle work for my girl." He mumbled, never taking his eyes off the positive pregnancy test on his phone screen.

"Wait. Wait. Wait. You losing me Capone. What you mean *my* little sister work for *your* girl?" she asked anxiously.

Everything was happening so fast. Capone couldn't register everything at once. How did Danielle end up tied with Pip? But most importantly, how the hell did Pip end up pregnant with his baby?

Danielle opened her eyes, immediately not recognizing her surroundings before it hit her. She was still laying on Nike's couch, the last place she remembered being yesterday. Slightly sitting up, Dani looked around for her phone before spotting it on the floor near her shoes. Leaning forward, Dani struggled to it grab it when she heard a door open and close.

"Good morning young lady." An older woman appeared from the back and spoke, dressed in navy blue scrubs.

"Hi-hey." Dani spoke back, staring at the woman who moved about the living room cleaning up.

After looking closely, she resembled Nike a lot, she must be his sister or something.

"Did my rude ass son offer you breakfast?" she stopped moving around and asked, now standing directly in front of Danielle.

Son, she repeated back to herself just when she heard another door open and close.

"Never mind, I see he just woke up himself." She smirked, grabbing the all-black purse that rested on the coffee table.

"I'm working a double. Don't fuck up my house Nike." His mother warned, placing a quick kiss on his cheek as he stood in the doorway rubbing his eyes.

Danielle looked on at their interaction and smiled. When Nike told her that he lived with his OG, she assumed that she was a deadbeat like Melissa, but she was proven to be wrong.

"Aye, we got some cereal in there if you want a bowl. I heard my OG in here talking shit." He said, locking the door behind his mom before heading into the kitchen.

"She's so cute." Dani replied, referring to his mother who looked no older than thirty.

"She aight. Her ass always working. I'm surprised she even came home last night." Nike stated, snatching the full ashtray off the wooden coffee table in front of them.

"Speaking of last night. What happened?" Dani probed, trying to recollect the events from the night before.

"Ohhhhhhh….. yo ass tried to stomp with the big dogs, that's what happened. You smoked one blunt with me and you tapped out."

Danielle laughed at how animated Nike was, prancing around the room. With him helping to jog her memory, everything started to become clearer. Nike ended up sweating Pip for Danielle's phone number. Since Nike was her Godbrother and she loved him to death, Pip gave up Danielle's information quicker than a snitch on *The First 48*. Catching her off guard, Nike offered to take her out to eat, in which, Danielle accepted his invitation. Taking her to some new jerk place out South, the two of them enjoyed their time together so much, they ended up back at Nike's house smoking. Admitting that she's never smoke weed before, Nike coached her through it, eventually coaching her into a marijuana coma.

"I stayed the night. Mecca gon' flip." Dani stated, grabbing her phone, pressing the side button to turn it on.

"My shit must be dead." She hissed, searching around looking for an outlet and charger.

"Nah, you dropped yo shit in the toilet last night." He informed her, walking over to the couch with a large bowl of Frosted Flakes.

"IN THE TOLIET? WHAT TYPE OF WEED YOU GIVE ME?" She yelled at him with bucked eyes.

"If I would have laced your shit, you woulda woke up sore with ya back blown out." He laughed but Danielle didn't find the joke funny.

"Aight look… you raced me in the house, we both had to pee. After cheating and pushing me to the side. Yo silly ass….."

"Dropped my phone…. I remember." She cut him off, stating.

Danielle thought back and began to remember more and more. She had so much fun with Nike, and he was truly an asshole; but for some reason, she was attracted to that.

"So ya moms don't trip about you having girls spending the night?" Danielle wanted to know, standing to her feet stretching.

"I told you, her ass ain't never here cuz she always working but nah, she don't say shit. Actually, you the first girl that slept on the couch. I keep the hoes in the backroom with me." Nike joked, but Danielle knew he was as serious as a heart attack.

"Anyway, let me get up and head home. I know my sister about to have a brain aneurysm. The bathroom this way again, right?" she asked, pointing towards the back of the house.

Without waiting for confirmation, Danielle headed in that direction, stumbling across the bathroom. After releasing herself and giving herself a few looks over in the mirror, she washed her hands and exited.

"I'm ready, let's ride." Nike said, standing by the door in the same jeans from last night and an Adidas hoodie.

Checking her pockets and bra to make sure she had everything, she left out the door before him, heading to his car.

"So, you say you only nineteen, right?" Dani asked, recalling to a conversation they had previously.

"Yeah, why you asked me that?" Nike questioned her questioning him before hitting the locks on his gray Jag.

"You just don't seem like the typical nineteen- year- old, that's all." She admitted, getting into the car, tugging at the seatbelt.

"I'on even know what that supposed to mean." He chuckled before stepping inside himself.

"Like, ya moms work a normal job, yet y'all crib nice but not *millionaire* nice, no offense…" She paused, noticing the stern look on Nike's face.

"You young as hell driving a Jag with all this jewelry and nice shit. I need answers." She continued, looking back at him straight in the eyes.

It was like the two of them was having the most intense, *don't blink contest*, when Nike cracked a smile, displaying a perfect set of teeth.

"Damn gurl, you nosey as fuck. Why you so nosey Dani?" he twisted his head to the side and asked, still displaying those perfect thirty-twos.

"Boy…. Boy …… Boy whatever," she waved him off before staring straight ahead out the window.

Stopping at the red light, Nike turned the radio up while Danielle shifted in her seat, now facing out the side window.

"OH MY FUCKING GOD!" She yelled just as the light turned green, her head spinning in the direction they had just left.

"What? You good shorty?" Nike turned down the radio, asking frantically.

"Yeah…. I---I----I just saw someone I knew." She stuttered, remembering the look in Dame's eyes the moment he realized it was her.

"You sure. You good? Want me to hit the block?" he offered, ready to switch lanes.

Sitting back in her seat, Danielle struggled to get the image of Dame of out her brain. It had been so long since she had last seen him. She knew he didn't drop off the face of the Earth. She figured Capone scared him away, that or he was in jail. Honestly, Danielle wished he was dead, but her dreams had been completely crushed.

"I'm straight. You ain't gotta go back around." She finally replied, her mood completely thrown off.

Pulling in front of the condo, Nike double parked, letting Danielle out at the door.

"Imma see you tonight at the strip club, right?" he asked, hitting the locks for her.

"Yeah, I'll be there." She replied with an assuring smile.

Blowing her an air kiss, Danielle rolled her eyes, closed the car door, completely ignoring him. She tried her best to play her role but found herself smiling from ear to ear before she made it to the curb. Sliding her key into the door, Danielle immediately noticed that the house was quiet, which was the first indication that Mecca wasn't there. Heading straight to the bathroom, Danielle wasted no time turning on the shower and hopping in. After washing up twice, she rinsed off carefully, trying not to get her braids wet. Scooping her belongings up off the floor, she headed to the bedroom, wrapped in a towel. Flying across the bed like Superman, Danielle landed in the middle and closed her eyes. She loved to air dry but had absolutely no intentions on falling asleep.

The sound of an ambulance passing by awoke Dani from her slumber. She could tell how dark the room had gotten that it was late. Sitting up and adjusting her towel, Danielle looked around for her phone, spotting it on the nightstand. Standing to her feet, she instantly flopped back down, remembering that it was broke. Grabbing the remote control, she turned to the Guide channel where it informed her that it as a quarter until nine. Really jumping up now, Danielle ran over to her closet, pulling out the outfit Stephany helped her pick out.

Wearing a pair of a black distressed ripped up jeans, with huge holes at the thighs, she matched it up with an off the shoulder Chanel top that she still couldn't believe she paid so much money for. After sliding into her Yeezy's, Danielle headed into the bathroom where she fixed her edges. Running back into the room, she checked the TV for the time again and then turned it off.

Stephany was set to pull up at nine-thirty and it was three minutes passed that. Knowing they had no way of communicating, Danielle decided to wait in the lobby of their building. Pulling up about four minutes later, Dani jumped in the car with Steph and headed to Fantasy's Gentleman Club.

The night was early, and the line was already wrapped around the corner when they pulled up. Stepping out the car, Dani made sure Stephany's whip was valet parked before they entered. Heading to the front of the line, Danielle spoke to Chuck, one of Pip's security guards before he let the two of them through.

"THIS BITCH CRACKING ALREADY!" Stephany yelled in Danielle's ear as soon as they hit the main floor.

Shaking her head up and down to the beat and agreeing with her friend, Dani's eyes roamed the crowd, looking for familiar faces. After spotting a few of Pip's girls, Danielle told Steph to go to the bar and that she'll meet her there in a few minutes. Walking off in the opposite direction of Stephany, Danielle headed towards the women's bathroom, where she saw Troy going. Due to the million bitches in there and the four stalls in the bathroom, the line was extremely long.

"Hey Troy, how you doing?" Danielle appeared from behind her and asked, causing her neck to snap in her direction.

"Oh hey Dani, I'm good, how you been?" she asked with a warm smile.

"I can't complain. Have you seen Pip?"

"Not sense earlier, ask Brandy, that was the last person I seen her with." Troy advised.

Thanking her for the information, Danielle ended the conversation, in search for Pip. Turning the corner on her way back, Danielle collided with a familiar face.

"Waddup shorty?" Nike leaned in and said close enough to make the hairs on the back of her neck stand.

"Hey. You seen Pip?" she asked, trying to avoid the uneasy feeling she got around him.

"Yeah, I seen her talking to that nigga Mac over by the DJ booth but check the back." He insisted.

Dismissing herself the same way she had just done with Troy, Danielle was now on her way to the back office, the place she should have checked first. Knocking on the door, Danielle waited a few seconds before letting herself in. She was unsure if her knocks could be heard over the loud music, and she didn't want to be standing out there for no reason. Walking inside, she noticed the office was empty, just as she was about to turn around, she heard noise coming from the bathroom. Headed towards the noise, she raised her hand to knock on the door when it opened.

"Oh my bad Brandy. I thought Pip was in here."

"You good?" Dani asked, noticing the streaks of tears in Brandy's make up.

"Girl move, it ain't like you care." Brandy hissed, stepping around Dani, leaving her facing a closed door.

"Girl, I ain't about to kiss yo ass....FUCK YOU!" Danielle cursed, sticking up her middle finger.

"Exactly….. like I said, you don't care. Yo lil young and dumb ass better be careful while you so thirsty to take my spot." Brandy ranted before tossing back the opened Hennessy bottle.

"I know that's what you THINK, but bitch, I ain't trying to beef with a bitch about another bitch. That shit gay. I'm trying to get money and stay out the way." Danielle schooled her.

Brandy smacked her lips before trying to walk off but she stumbled, wasting some of the brown liquor on the floor.

"You drunk as fuck. You need to take it easy." Danielle said, helping her to her feet.

"Thank you." Brandy mumbled, slowly yanking away, gaining her composure.

Taking another big gulp of the Hennessy, Danielle shook her head. Brandy was taking the term, *"drive the boat"* too far.

"Look, I just came looking for Pip, have you seen her?" Danielle questioned, ready to move on from the situation.

"Last I seen was her, she talking to my baby daddy," Brandy informed her while rolling her eyes to the back of her head.

"Baby daddy? I wasn't aware that you had kids." Dani replied with a puzzled look on her face.

"Nobody knows." She whispered, rubbing her flat stomach.

Danielle's eyes shifted from Brandy's stomach to the bottle of Henny she was drinking like water. She wasn't acting like she was with child but then again, that was none of her business.

"Congratulations but can you tell me who exactly you seen her with?"

"Mac…"

"Wait. Who?" Dani asked, trying to ensure she heard her correctly.

"Yup." Brandy confirmed it, taking another swig.

"But I thought that was her man…Never mind."

Danielle stood their stunned, wondering what type of freaky shit did they have going on. She was almost positive that Mac belonged to Pip, but Brandy had just confused her.

"I will nevvveeerrrrr."

Danielle's eyes bucked at the sight of Brandy who stood there crying uncontrollably. Taken back by her actions, Dani was unsure of what to do.

"Maybe….."

"Maybe *nothing*, Dani. I know what I'm talking about. That lady knows how I feel about that man, yet she's always smiling in his face. I love Pip like a big sister and thanks to her, I've made a lot of money, but this shit not worth my sanity." Brandy spoke as she cried like a baby.

"Have you…."

"I'm thinking about seeing a therapist and shit. I'm going crazy because of this bitch. I can't sleep at night. Every time I close my eyes, I see that baby's face." Brandy cut her off and stated.

"Baby?"

"Yes baby! I'm not sure why she'll even do this to me, knowing the secrets I hold for her."

Brandy was on a full drunken rant, spilling all the tea. From the outside looking in, no one would be able to tell she felt the way she did, which is why Danielle was still shocked.

"Then poor Capone…"

"CAPONE? CAPONE WHO?" Danielle yelled, even causing Brandy to jump.

"Oh, that's Pip's boyfriend. He's heavy in these streets, you may know him. That man has no clue how she really is. She's so insecure when it comes to him, but I'm convinced he's a good man."

Brandy's tea was overflowing everywhere. There was no way possible that the world was this small and Pip and Capone was *actually* in a relationship.

"The day she hit and killed that little boy, she was stalking Capone because she heard he was on 16th and Trumbull with a bitch."

Danielle's world stopped moving, her ears began to ring, and her heart began to ache. 16th and Trumbull was the block that Coby was hit and killed on and thinking back on that fateful day, Capone was out there talking to Mecca.

"Aye Brandy, what did you just say about a little boy being hit?" Danielle swallowed the lump in her throat and asked.

"A few months back, Pip was speeding down the street, didn't see the speed hump, lost control of the car, and hit a little boy. The baby died and Pip said out her mouth how she didn't care and she'll never be caught…. crazy ass bitch!" Brandy chuckled, taking another swig of the almost gone Henny.

Chapter One

"MECCCCAAAAA!!! MECCCCAAAAA!!"

Danielle's loud screams scared the shit out of Mecca, causing her to jump out her sleep. Clutching her invisible pearls, Mecca scanned the room, after noticing it was empty and assuming it was a dream, she slowly laid back down when her bedroom door swung open.

"MECCA!" Danielle yelled again, causing Mecca to sit back up.

Watching Danielle flick the light on and then off again, Mecca wondered what the emergency was, when in fact, she was the one with all the questions for her little sister.

"Damn, is the house on fire again? Bitch what's your problem?" a calm Mecca asked, checking the time on her phone.

"I need you to wake up and wake up now. I got some shit to tell you." Dani panicked causing Mecca's mind to race.

She hadn't heard from Danielle in twenty-four hours and after her and Capone's discovery, she had a few words of her own to say.

"What Danielle? What is it?"

Danielle fixed the covers on Mecca's bed before taking a sit on the edge. By the way she was breathing, it was obvious that she was trying to catch her breath.

"Ok so look right….. Remember I told you that I work for….."

"Capone's bitch Pip…. Yeah I know." Mecca cut her off mid-sentence and explained.

"Wait? How you know?" Danielle swung her head around and quizzed.

"Because I found a business card in your room earlier and Capone was here to confirm it." Mecca elaborated.

"Oh ok but there's more to the story, just listen. I met Pip the night I lost the baby. She broke up the fight and kinda been around the whole time. Seeing something in me, she offered me a position with her company, that's how I ended up working for her…."

"Does she know you my sister?" Mecca interrupted and asked pulling the flower sheets off of her.

"No, I didn't know she knew Capone until today. I thought her nigga was this dude name Mac." Dani continued, causing Mecca's mouth to drop.

"Wait. Mac is Capone's best friend." Mecca advised her as the story began to heat up.

"I JUST found that out too now stop cutting me off and listen."

Danielle cleared her throat before telling Mecca everything, from the top to the bottom, making sure not to leave out one detail.

"WAIT! STOP! So you telling me that you actually work for a brothel and not an interior design company?" Mecca pondered, cutting her off again, ensuring that she heard her right.

"Blew my fuckn mind too but let's fast forward to tonight. She was having this secretive party tonight at Mac's club. I get there and I'm looking all around for the bitch, I couldn't find her, but I ran into the bitch Brandy."

"Now that's the lil bitch who be hating on you, right?" Mecca asked, making sure she was keeping up.

Nodding her head up and down, yes, Mecca allowed Danielle to continue the story.

"Turns out, she low key bitter. I caught the hoe at vulnerable state, she was drunk and off a pill spilling all the tea."

"Gurl, what tea? Keep going?" Mecca encouraged, fully woke and ready to hear the rest.

A part of her was pissed that Danielle, once again moved around like a thief in the night, sneaky but she was happy that she was finally coming clean.

"So, this bitch proceeds to tell me that not only is Pip fucking Mac…."

"SHUT THE FUCK UP BITCH!" Mecca jumped to her feet and yelled.

"But so is Brandy and she's pregnant by him!"

"Wait? Who pregnant by him?" a confused Mecca stopped rejoicing and asked.

"Not Pip but Brandy, that aint even it but I need you to sit down before I tell you the last part."

Noticing the serious look in Danielle's eyes, Mecca slowly sat down, prepping herself for whatever it was she was about to hear.

"During Brandy's drunken rant, she revealed that she was in the car one day when Pip hit and killed a little boy…… that little boy being Coby."

"Danielle stop fucking playing with me. Bitch it aint April, stop playing." Mecca stood up and replied, waving Dani's silly ass off.

There was no way in hell Pip was the bitch that killed her little brother. The world was small, and Chicago was even smaller, but she knew damn well what she was hearing couldn't be true.

"I wish it was an April's Fool joke but it's not. Brandy said that Pip was stalking Capone, something she did often. She was riding down our block, trying to catch him talking to you when she hit him. Brandy said the bitch kept going like nothing happened. Even bragging about not getting caught."

"I --- need--- my --- asthma pump." Mecca struggled to say as she felt her chest caving in.

Born with severe asthma, Mecca had been able to control her attacks the older she got, however, there was still some things that triggered a flare up, Danielle's confession, being one.

"Where is it?" Danielle jumped to her feet and asked, scanning the semi-dark room with her eyes.

Watching her flick on the light, Mecca began to wreck her brain, trying to figure out where she last had it, since it had been so long since she used it. Drawing a blank, she became more anxious which made it even harder to breath.

"I—do----don't know." She struggled to say as she tried to mentally coach herself, but it was no use.

"I'm calling an ambulance, look at you, you can't breathe." Dani panicked, grabbing Mecca's phone.

Mecca hated hospitals and dreaded going there but she honestly couldn't breathe she tried to take deep breaths, which usually worked but she wasn't so lucky now.

"They on their way. Let's head downstairs."

Dani helped Mecca move about the room gathering her things. She still couldn't believe that she was having an asthma attack, especially at that very moment. There was so many unanswered questions. She really needed Danielle to start from the top again, just to be completely sure she heard her correctly.

As soon as they made it to the lobby, the ambulance was pulling up. Thankful for that, especially seeing how she felt like she was dying. Mecca did everything the paramedics requested of her, making the ride to the hospital a smooth one.

Dani stayed right there by her side, holding her hand and all, like they did in the movies. Mecca could tell by the look on Danielle's face that her mind was everywhere, and had they not been around strangers, she would've had her continue the story. After the short ride, Mecca was rushed inside to the triage area where the nurses asked a thousand questions, while giving her a treatment. Once her breathing was under control, Mecca was assigned a room and Danielle wasn't far behind her.

"So Mecca, when you and Capone discovered I worked for Pip, he didn't tell you right then and there she was into some modern day prostitution type shit." Dani asked, sliding her chair closer to the bed.

"Nope, the nigga aint said shit. How you motherfuckers walking around like the shit normal." Mecca quizzed, taking a sip from the small cup of orange juice.

"To be honest sis, that man might not even know. When I say Brandy made this bitch sound like Cruella De Vil, I mean that shit. Like, low key, now that I sit back and think about it, the bitch did act a little looney." Dani ranted, pulling Mecca in with each word.

The shit sounded like a Tyler Perry Movie to Mecca, she was still in disbelief. If Capone did know that her sister was involved in some type of prostitution ring and didn't tell her, right then and there, Mecca was going to be pissed. If the nigga really didn't know how his bitch got down, then that was another story, a truly sad one.

"Danielle, look in my bag and hand me my phone, I think it's ringing." Mecca requested as Dani stood to her feet, heading over towards the radiator.

Mecca watched Dani's facial expression change as she handed her the vibrating phone. Looking down at the screen, Capone's name flashed across with a few emojis attached.

"You gon' answer?" Danielle questioned, heading back to her seat.

"Yeah, I gotta know if this nigga know…."

Pressing the green circle, accepting the call, Mecca let out a deep sigh before shaking her head.

"Hello" she drily spoke, sitting up in the uncomfortable hospital bed.

"You good?" his deep voice asked from the other end.

"Yeah, I --- ummm --- had an asthma attack and the ambulance had to…."

"What hospital you at?" he quickly cut her off and asked, just as Mecca placed the call on speaker.

"I'm good Capone I---"

"WHAT HOSPITAL YOU AT?" he yelled, causing Mecca and Danielle to look at each other and smirk.

"I'm at Northwestern but….."

"I'm on my way…."

Capone ended the call, leaving both sisters looking at each other speechless. Just as Mecca opened her mouth to speak, her phone began ringing/vibrating again. Assuming it was Capone calling with a question, Mecca flipped the phone over, noticing in fact it was a Facetime from Kool. Without thinking twice AND forgetting where she was at, Mecca fixed her hair before answering the call.

"Who is that?" Danielle whispered as they waited for the call to connect.

The service in the hospital was horrible and the Wi-fi they had was bootlegged.

"Kool." Mecca smiled but that smile quickly faded away when she noticed the look on Danielle's face.

"Why would you answer, knowing….."

"What up baby? Kool's smooth voice drowned out Dani's words.

Knowing now that she had fucked up, Mecca knew there was no way to play it off.

"Where you at?" You at the hospital?" his voice elevated, noticing Mecca's background.

"I'm good baby, I just had a little asthma attack, as a matter of fact, I'm about to get discharged now." She lied, cutting her eyes at Danielle who covered her own mouth and laughed.

"Aw word, what hospital?" he questioned, seeming a bit calmer.

"Northwestern." She honestly replied.

"Aight well, that discharge shit can take a minute. I'm on my way up there to sit with you and take you home."

Kool didn't wait for Mecca to reply before ending the call, leaving the sisters speechless for the second time that night.

Chapter Two

"Aye, let get forty on pump seven." Capone requested, sliding the gas station attendant two twenty-dollar bills before walking away.

As he headed towards the door, he noticed a woman walking in wearing a black jumpsuit. Holding the door open, she thanked him with a smile before breezing pass him. Glancing briefly at her ass, Capone headed out the door and towards his car. Pulling the gas nozzle out of its compartment, Capone selected premium and began fueling his Porsche. Scanning the parking lot, his eyes landed at the door, where shorty in the jumpsuit peeked her head out.

"Aye Kool, what type of pop you want?" she screamed, just as the windows on a black Jeep began to roll down.

"Get me a water." Kool's deep voice replied behind the dark tint in the ride.

Capone had to do a double take to make sure he was seeing right and his thoughts were confirmed, it was Mecca's homie Kool. Although he had only seen him a few times, he had a distinctive name in the hood and Capone never forgot a face.

After he finished pumping his gas, Capone got back to his car and headed towards the hospital. It was the wee hours in the morning, but the streets were full of partygoers headed home or to the after-hour spot of their choice. Capone was headed in too before he spoke with Mecca and discovered she was at the hospital. Although she made it clear that she was straight, Capone still needed to see for himself.

Snatching the blunt out of the cupholder, Capone sparked it up as he replayed the events of the day in his head. On top of finding out that Mecca's little sister Dani worked for Pip and Pip claims of being pregnant, the day was a day to remember.

Between the hard pulls from the blunt and Capone's mind racing, he was pulling into a parking spot across the street from the hospital before he knew it. Killing the engine, he headed in through the emergency room doors where he was greeted by a security guard. After giving him all the information that he had, the older gray bearded man escorted Capone to the back rooms where Mecca could be found. Knocking lightly on the door, Capone let himself when he heard laughter spilling from the other end.

"What the fuck so funny?" he asked, drawing both Mecca and Danielle's eyes towards him.

"What up Capone?" Danielle giggled, followed by Mecca who spoke after her.

Walking over to a chair near the radiator, Capone couldn't help but notice how gorgeous Mecca looked even laying there in a hospital bed. He found it crazy at how much he was attracted to her now, compared to before. Mecca always had a cute face and shape, it was just that now, Capone seen so much more in her.

"I'm thirsty, imma go find a vending machine or sum. I'll be back." Danielle stood to her feet and stated, dismissing herself, leaving Capone and Mecca alone.

Silence fell upon the room the moment she left. Capone could tell by the way Mecca tried to avoid eye contact with him that something was on her mind.

"So, what the doctor's saying?" he finally broke the silence and asked.

Capone watched Mecca shift in her seat and adjust the flat pillows before looking over in his direction. After staring at each other oddly for a few more seconds, she finally answered him.

"I'm cool. I just needed a treatment and they sending me home with a new asthma pump so I'll be straight."

Mecca's tone was different, something Capone noticed the moment she opened her mouth. He knew the situation that occurred earlier put them in a strange predicament, but it was nothing they couldn't get passed. Capone hadn't even had the chance to confront Pip about Danielle being employed with her, but he had every intention to.

"What's wrong shorty, talk to me?" Capone stated, standing to his feet, heading over towards her.

He watched Mecca's eyes shift from him to the floor, the closer he got. After getting the text message about being pregnant from Pip, Capone left without saying anything else to Mecca. He was confused about their discovery and even more confused about Pip and the pregnancy situation. He had yet to address anything, but he knew avoiding it was a bad idea.

"You talked to Dani about work yet?" he eased closer to her and quizzed, trying to see exactly where her head was at.

"Yeah a little bit but she had no clue that Pip was connected to you, which makes me wonder if Pip was aware of the connection?" Mecca replied with questioning eyes.

Capone's mind instantly began to race, did Pip have an ulterior motive for hiring Danielle but if that was the case, where did these motives come from? Sure, Mecca was brought up a few times amongst the couple but not enough for Pip to be on no sneaky shit. Capone honestly hoped and prayed that it was a coincidence because if not, a lot of shit was about to go left.

"Capone, let me ask you a question."

Mecca's voice grabbed his full attention, as he had begun to drift off thinking about the connection amongst the circle.

"What's up?" he looked over at her and said, just as there was a knock at the door.

Both of their eyes landed on Danielle who was entering with a bag of chips in one hand and a pack of M&Ms in the other.

"Sorry, was I interrupting something? Need me to come back?" Danielle asked, her eyes shifting back and forth between Capone and Mecca.

"Nah shorty you good." Capone chuckled, heading back over to his seat.

Although there was a conversation that definitely needed to be had, Capone realized that now was not the best time, so he decided to wait.

"As a matter of fact, we were talking about you. I told Capone how you knew nothing about him, and that lady being connected." Mecca followed behind him and explained, filling Danielle in.

Capone shook his head up and down in agreement as she spoke. He too had a few questions of his own for Danielle but just like the other issues, now was not the time discuss them. Glancing at the time on his phone, Capone noticed it was almost four in the morning. Although he was tired, he wanted to make sure Mecca was good before he left and headed home. He also was debating back and forth with himself about whether or not he should tell Mecca about him spotting Kool and some woman at the gas station. Snitching was never in Capone's blood, but neither was allowing some nigga to play Mecca. There was no question in his mind that'll he'll kill for Mecca, the same way he would Diamond, the only difference was, Mecca wasn't his sister, nor did he look at her like she was.

"Look, I'm about to…."

Capone stood to his feet and said stretching, before letting out a long yarn that caused him to pause. Just as he was about to finish his statement, there was another knock on the door.

"I hope this these people telling me I can go home." Mecca rejoiced, sitting up straight in the hospital bed.

After giving the person on the other end permission to enter, Capone watched as the door swung up and in walked Kool.

"What's up baby? You good?" he asked, mugging Capone before going over to Mecca's bed, where he placed a kiss on her lips.

"I'm good bae--- Kool. I told you that you aint have to come." She replied nervously, cutting her eyes at Capone who still was standing and staring.

"I told you that I was coming. What up Danielle? What up homie!" Kool looked over at Capone and spoke before directing his attention back to Mecca.

Giving a slight head nod, Capone patted his pockets for his phone and keys before walking off towards the door.

"Imma holler at you later Mecca. See you Dani." Capone stated before making his exit out of the hospital room.

Chapter Three

Pip sat in the living room with all the lights off, waiting for Capone to make his entrance. It was almost five in the morning and he still hadn't made it home. It was early morning after her party and although she was just making it in herself, he had no reason to be out, especially since he wasn't present at the club. Noticing the bright headlights in the driveway, she knew it was Capone finally arriving. Siting up comfortable on the cream leather sectional couch, Pip crossed her legs, anxiously anticipating his arrival. Luckily for her, she didn't have to wait long, Capone came in rapping the latest Da Baby, bobbing his head up and down like he didn't have a care in this world. Pip couldn't believe the nigga had the audacity to scroll in like nothing was wrong. Standing up to her feet, Pip slowly walked over to the wall, where she flicked on the light, causing Capone to stop his stride.

"Just the person I need to talk to. I'm glad you up baby." He said nonchalantly as he headed into the kitchen.

Pip stared him down like a hawk as he went inside the refrigerator and pulled out a bottle of water. He must of felt her eyes on him because he turned around and faced her, giving off a fake smile.

"You want one?" he asked, holding the Aquafina water bottle in the hair.

"Nah I'm good but what you can tell is, why the fuck you coming in the house so late. You might as well had breakfast and lunch with the bitch." Pip snapped, walking closer to Capone, never breaking their stare.

Pip watched Capone smirk before gulping down the rest of the water. He then finally closed the fridge before walking over to the garbage where he tossed the plastic bottle in the bin. Taking his hands and running them across his waves, Pip watched Capone lock eyes with her again before he came and stood in front of her.

"My homie had an asthma attack and I was at the hospital. How was ladies night?" he asked, staring deep into her eyes like he was searching for the truth.

Almost forgetting her own lie, Pip was relieved that Capone spoke on it first and rejogged her memory.

"Ladies night was cool but let's not circle around the issue. What friend was in the hospital and why you aint even call me?" she questioned, shifting her weight to one side and placing her hands on her hips.

"Mecca but…."

"Not this bitch AGAIN Capone. I'm almost convinced you fucking this bitch" she threw both hands in the air and yelled.

"If you wanna have this conversation, you need to calm the fuck down but if I was fucking Mecca, I wouldn't be here with you right now. But since we on Mecca, why Danielle working for you?"

Pip knew her ears had to be deceiving her, how did Capone know about Dani and what the fuck did Mecca have to do with it?

"Dani? What Dani gotta do with this and most importantly, what the fuck does Dani have to do with that bitch Mecca?" Pip replied, anxiously waiting on his explanation.

Pip's plan to stay up and confront Capone didn't consist of him turning shit around and questioning her. She really needed to know how he knew Dani and she needed to know now.

"Ava, stop with the dumb shit. Do you or do you not have an employee by the name of Danielle Young?"

"Yes I do but…."

"What's the odds of you hiring Dani and Dani and Mecca being sisters?"

"SISTERS! WHO THE FUCK SISTERS?" Pip screamed, knowing damn well like hell, she hadn't just heard him correctly.

"Look, I aint know shit about Dani and Mecca being tied together. Keep in mind, I don't know shit about Mecca, well only the small details you've told me." She replied truthfully, her mind beginning to wonder.

Pip watched Capone walk away from her, heading to the living room, where he flicked on the light. He then headed over to the bookshelf where he grabbed the tin can that contained his stash of weed. Not being a smoker herself, Pip needed to hit the blunt in order for her mind to register what Capone was saying.

"So you aint know huh?" he walked back over to her and asked again, this time breaking down the blunt.

"NOOOOOO! The fuck I gotta lie for?" she rolled her ass, taking a seat on the stool at the kitchen counter.

"If this Mecca bitch walked past me right now, I wouldn't know who she was." Pip continued, semi telling the truth.

She would for sure without a doubt know the bitch if she walked past but what she really meant was, she only knew of her and outside of that one face to face encounter, she really wouldn't know then.

"I don't know, all this shit sound weird to me but it aint adding up, this world aint never that small." Capone spoke, drying the freshly rolled blunt with a lighter.

The world was definitely that small and Pip couldn't believe just how small it was herself. If in fact Dani and Mecca was related, that meant Mecca knew the truth behind Pip's House and it could get back to Capone, if it hadn't already.

"Since yall discussing me and shit. What else was said?" she quizzed, with attempts on getting more out of Capone but it didn't work.

"What more is there to know?" he exhaled the smoke out of his mouth and asked, looking her directly in the eyes.

Capone's stares caused goosebumps to form on Pip's smooth skin and the small hairs on the back of her neck to stand. Was he being truthful, or did he know more and was waiting on her to come clean? Either way it went, she couldn't chance it, Dani and Mecca knew too much, which meant they both had to go!

Chapter Four

Danielle stood near the curb outside of school talking to five girls when Mecca pulled up in one of Kool's cars, blasting Cardi B's latest album. Everyone rapped along like they were at a concert while some bystanders struggled to see who was behind the tints.

"Damn G, that's yo sister Mecca?" Amber, another senior asked Dani as she too tried to see inside the Tesla.

"Yeah." She replied, placing both bookbag straps on her shoulders before stepping towards the car.

"So Dani, you want us to call you when again?" Lynette asked this time from her spot in the grass.

"I'll let you know, as a matter of fact, since I got a new phone, I'll put it in a group chat." Danielle replied, assuring the ladies that she'll stay in touch.

After saying their final goodbyes, Dani jumped in the car with Mecca who was just wrapping up a phone call with Diamond.

"How was school? Put ya seatbelt on." Mecca asked and demanded at the same time.

"School was cool. How was class for you?" Dani replied, adjusting the seatbelt around her chest.

"It was straight. I see you got a fan club now." Mecca laughed, referring to the girls crowed around Danielle.

"Girl bye! I wouldn't call it a fan club."

"What you call it then? It's a far cry from your popularity last year." Mecca noted, forcing Danielle to remember her Junior year.

Mecca was absolutely right; it was a far cry from last year but then again everything in their life lately had been different from previous years. Danielle was beyond happy that things were looking up for them, she just needed to make sure it stayed that way.

"Aye, you talked to that bitch Pip yet?" Mecca looked over at Danielle and asked with a frown on her face.

It had been four days since everything came to the surface and Dani hadn't spoken to Pip. In fact, that's the way she wanted things to stay until her and Mecca decided what they wanted to do with the information they had.

"I say we just ride up on the bitch and beat her ass, I mean that wouldn't get us justice for Coby but……"

"And we'll be dead before the next morning. As bad as EYE wanna beat the bitch ass, it aint that simple. I told you, Pip's family tied to some type of mob shit." Danielle replied, trying to explain to Mecca that things were as simple as they seemed.

The roles were reversed, Mecca was the one ready to shoot and ask questions later when in actuality, it was Danielle who really acted that way. Dani understood that Mecca was hurt and ready to do damage, but Danielle had other plans. Plans that would put them in a better position for life.

"I was thinking, how about I play it cool, see how far I can get in and then get revenge."

"Get in? Get in where and do what? I'm lost." Mecca replied with a puzzle look on her face just as they pulled to a stop sign.

"Just hear me out. Beating Pip's ass wouldn't solve shit and although killing her would be ideal, there's another way to hurt the bitch." Danielle explained as she stared out the window at the leaves on the ground.

"What other way?" Mecca mumbled under her breath before pulling back in the flow of traffic.

"I want the bitch wealth. I want everything she has, that bitch owes us." Danielle fumed, thinking about the loss they took at the hands of Pip.

Twisting her head in the direction of Mecca, Danielle noticed her shaking her head up and down as if she agreed.

"I love the idea but let's be real Dani, this aint the movies, how the fuck two young, BROKE young chicks like ourselves gon' do some shit like that? I mean, let's think realistically, we…."

"REALISTICALLY, we can do whatever the fuck we wanna do Mecca. Look at us now, look how far we've come. With the right tools and outlets, we can make some big shit happen Mecca but I gotta know you with me." Dani cut her off in mid-sentence and explained.

"I'm with you but…."

"And being with me means that YOU have to trust me. I know Bad Ass Mecca use to taking the lead but you gotta hop in the passenger seat with this one and let me drive the boat."

Again, Mecca remained quiet, instead, she shook her head up and down while staring at the road ahead. Not only was Dani pleased that Mecca agreed, she was shocked. Mecca was always the mother and leader in every situation that involved them but she had no choice but to take the backseat on this one.

"Drop me off at the Subway down the street." Dani requested before Mecca made the right onto their block.

"It's food in the house why you…."

"I'm meeting someone there, just pull over, I'll be home in about an hour to fill you in."

Mecca did as request and pulled over, letting Danielle out the car and onto the curb. In addition to checking her surroundings, Danielle made sure her gun was secured before entering the restaurant. Walking inside, she immediately spotted Brandy at a table near the restrooms and headed over towards her.

"Thanks for meeting me so last minute." Dani approached the table with a smile and stated.

"No problem, I had a doctor's appointment around the corner, so I was in the neighborhood anyway." Brandy replied, opening up a bag of Ranch Doritos.

"Aw yeah that's right, checking on the little one. How far along are you?" Danielle quizzed, taking a seat across from her.

This was the first time the ladies had spoken since Brandy spilled all the tea about Pip. The way she had diarrhea at the mouth, Dani knew that she could use her in aid to getting revenge on Pip. There was nothing worse than a woman scorned and poor Brandy had the words printed on her forehead.

"I'm eight weeks." She replied in a low dry tone.

"What's wrong? You don't seem too happy?" Dani pried, displacing a concerned look on her face.

"I was until…. I was until Mac told me to get an abortion." Brandy lowered her head and admitted.

Danielle's mouth opened but she wasn't surprised, she was playing her role. Mac was a dog and anyone within a five-mile radius could see that. Not only was Brandy pregnant by him, Mecca said his woman Ashley was too and to make matters worse, Pip was fucking him as well.

"Look, I know we not friends but I'm sorry you even gotta go through that. Does Pip know you pregnant?" Dani quizzed, looking her straight in the eyes.

"Dani, Pip is the one who hooked me up with Mac. At the time when we started fucking around; me, her, Capone and Mac were hanging out tough. I know about Ashlee and everything but let Pip tell is, their relationship was rocky." Brandy explained, finally locking eyes with Danielle from across the table.

"That's crazy…."

"And now every time I look up, she in his face." An angry Brandy cut off Danielle and added in.

"Damn, that's fucked up, but can I tell you something. A secret, you can't tell nobody." Danielle leaned forward and whispered, praying to Petty Gods that she falls for the bait.

Dani watched Brandy's eyes light up like a Christmas tree as she eagerly waited to hear what was next. Truth was, Danielle didn't have any real information, however she planned on using the little that she did have to wheel Brandy in.

"I know for a fact that Pip and Mac is fucking around. The first day she gave me your job, we went to the strip club. She had me waiting at the bar while the two of them went in the back to his office and fucked."

"I KNOW YOU FUCKING LYING!" Brandy banged her fist on the restaurants table and yelled, causing a few eyes to dart in their direction.

"I wish I was. Even when we got back in the car, she bragged about how good he ate pussy and blah blah blah." Danielle rambled on with her lies.

She knew Brandy would never have the balls to comfort Pip herself which meant she would walk around secretly hating her, which was exactly what Danielle needed to happen.

"Yeah I had no idea none of this was going on. I'm sorry Brandy."

Danielle reached across the table and softly caressed Brandy's hand as tears began to slide down her cheeks. Part of Dani actually felt sorry for the girl, Pip had yet again shown how ruthless and coldhearted she was. Wanting so badly to put a bullet between her eyes, Dani remained calm and played her role.

"So what you gon do?" Dani asked, catching Brandy off guard by the look on her face.

"What---What you mean?" she sniffed, using the back of her hand to wipe the tears away.

"About the baby with Mac. You gon get an abortion?" she questioned, curious to know the answer.

"When I was seven, I was raped by my step-dad. He raptured something in me and doctors said that I'll never be able to have kids." Brandy blurted out, leaving Danielle's mouth on the floor again, this time for real.

"I am so fuckn sorry to hear that. Trust me, I know the feeling you are feeling way too well but….."

Danielle paused to collect her thoughts. Hearing about Brandy's experience brought back unwanted memories of Dame rapping her and even more memories of Yana, who's around that age now.

"Like I said before, we not friends but…. I'm here if you need anything Brandy and I hate you even dealing with this bullshit."

Danielle spoke honestly and truthfully from the heart. She had read Brandy wrong all this time. She was simply being loyal to who she thought was a friend, or even mentor. Pip was a dirty bitch and all her lies and schemes were coming to surface.

"How long have you been around Pip?" Dani asked with attempts on changing the subject.

"I'm twenty-one now. Since I was seventeen." Brandy recalled, crumbling up the empty bag of chips.

Danielle had only been around for a few months and knew a lot, she could only imagine the type of vital information Brandy had been exposed to. Feeling her phone vibrate on the table, Brandy flipped it over, noticing a text message from Nike as well as one from an unfamiliar number. Smiling at the sight of his name on her screen,

Danielle read the message from him first before switching over to the unknown sender.

630-231-0213: Hey Dani, this is Diamond, Mecca's friend (Capone sister) …. I stole your number out of Mecca's phone. I know her birthday coming up and I wanted to do something special for her. I was thinking a surprise party, but I would need your help. You down?

Smiling at the phone harder than before, Danielle loved the idea of a surprise party for Mecca. She had never had a party, let alone a surprise one and if anybody deserved it, it was her sister. On top of all that they've been through, Mecca completed her first year in college on the Dean's List with a perfect GPA. A party would be the perfect gift and Dani couldn't wait to help start planning.

Shooting a text back, letting Diamond know she was down, Danielle directed her attention back on Brandy who looked spaced out.

"You good?" Dani asked, snapping Brandy out of whatever space cloud she was on.

"Yeah, my bad, just a lot on my mind, ya know." She replied, her eyes scanning the restaurant as if she was looking for someone.

"I get it but look, I gotta head up outta here. You have my number and if you need to talk about anything, just let me know." Danielle stated, standing to her feet.

"I appreciate it Danielle and I'm so sorry about what happened to your brother."

Stopping in her tracks, Danielle turned around, locking eyes with Brandy who sat in the same spot with more tears in her eyes.

"I was drunk as fuck the night I told you about the hit and run but not even a drunk mind could forget the hurt in your eyes the night I spilled the beans. I feel just as guilty as Pip because I should have gone to the authorities about it, but I didn't. I just pray to God I can redeem myself by telling you and although nothing will bring him back, I'm willing to do whatever it takes to help you get your OWN personal justice."

Chapter Five

Mecca allowed Kool's hands to guide her by the waist as she rode him slowly. Looking down and staring into his eyes, Mecca smiled as Kool bit down on his bottom lip. She couldn't front, the sensation she got from riding his dick was like nonother and she felt herself about to explode.

"Damn, slow down baby, you about to make me nut." He groaned lowly, suddenly closing his eyes.

Feeling herself about to reach her peak, Mecca ignored his warning and picked up the pace. It seemed the faster she went, the less it hurt, making the ride a much more pleasant one.

"I'mmmmm about to cum tooooo!!" she moaned out loud, tossing her head back as the sensation within her built.

Kool dug his nails into Mecca's skin as he too exploded, the both of them coming at the same time. Slowly getting up, her legs felt like noodles as she struggled to gain her balance. Flopping down on the bed on the side of him, Mecca turned over and laid on his chest as he stared at the ceiling.

"What you thinking about?" she quizzed, making invisible circles on his chest with her finger.

"I was thinking that you should move out of buddy crib and move in her with me and…."

"Baby pleaassseeee don't start this shit." She whined, already knowing where the conversation was headed.

Ever since Kool and Capone bumped heads at the hospital, Kool had been adamant about her moving out of his condo. Mecca understood why Kool felt the way he felt but things weren't as simple as he was trying to make them. Mecca wanted to move but she didn't want to move in with Kool, they had only been dating a few months and although he gave her everything she needed, she was not ready to make that move.

"I told you, I'm going to move when I find a place and besides, I would never leave Danielle."

"It's an extra room. I don't mind her being here. As a matter of fact, yall both can just stay until yall find another place but living in that nigga shit aint gon' cut it." He replied sternly, sitting up in the bed.

Following his lead, Mecca set up in the bed too, using the white sheets to aid in covering her naked body. She knew Kool had to frustrated, any man in their right mind would be pissed about their girl staying in another man house but he would have to just be pissed for the time being. Mecca and Dani hadn't come up with the perfect escape plan yet therefore, all parties involved had to be patient.

"Bae, I swear, give me another month and I'll be gone. Let me finish this semester out and then we can make arrangements, Ok?"

Kool turned around and faced Mecca who had a huge smile on her face. He made her so happy, and she planned on doing whatever it took to make him happy, even if that meant moving out of Capone's place.

"Imma start looking for a job so I can pay rent, that way…."

"Here you go with this job shit. Mecca just be cool and chill, I got you. Simply stay in school and anything you want, you can have." Kool assured her as the both of them climbed out of the bed.

Instead of verbally replying, Mecca headed to the bathroom with Kool's words resounding in her head. Both him and Capone had the same mentality when it came to her working, neither of them wanted her to. Forgetting her phone in the room, Mecca double back to grab it when she heard Kool on the phone.

"Yeah, that's one of the niggas blocks. I had Charlie peep it out but imma tell you like I told him, you muthafuckers need to make sure the shit is done and there are no witnesses around to talk.

Tripping on her own feet, Mecca bumped into the wall, causing Kool to stop talking.

"Imma hit you back later." He informed the person on the other end as Mecca reentered the room.

"Who you on the phone with?" she quizzed, looking at him sideways.

"Just work baby, I thought you was getting in the shower." He replied, standing to his feet and stretching.

"I am, I-I-forgot my phone." She stuttered, her eyes landing on his dick that still stood tall.

Round two immediately popped in her head, as her juices began to flow down her leg. Kool had a way of making her body feel good, it was as if he was personally made to please her. Snatching the phone off the charger, Mecca headed back out the room and towards the bathroom when the phone began to ring in her hands.

"Hello!" she answered, closing and locking the door behind her.

"I'm getting off the expressway, you almost ready?" Diamond asked as Mecca turned on the shower.

"Hopping in shower now, I'll be dressed by the time you get here." She informed her before ending the call.

Washing up in a hurry, Mecca handled all her business and was dressed and ready within fifteen minutes. It was about a thirty-minute drive for Diamond but seeing how she drove like a bat out of hell, Mecca knew not to underestimate her. Slipping on a pair of all-black Uggs, Mecca tossed on a black sweater dress from Fashion Nova to match, applied some curl custard lotion to her long locks and was ready to head out the door.

"Damn, where you going looking so good?" Kool snuck up behind her and asked as she stood in the mirror, giving herself one final overlook.

"Diamond wanna do some shopping. I guess we gon' grab something to eat too." She informed him before turning around and placing a soft kiss on his lips.

Mecca and Kool participated in a brief make out session before he pulled back, forcing her eyes to lock on his.

"Aye Mecca, I love you!" Kool spoke, those three little words piercing through Mecca's heart.

"I love you too baby." She replied with a huge smile, meaning every word.

She did love Kool and maybe she didn't realize it until now, but she knew for a fact that she did. He made her so happy but on top of all that, he made her feel special, something that only Madea and Capone were only able to do.

"This Diamond, I'll be back over here once we done." She announced, showing him the ringing phone in her hand.

Sharing one more passionate kiss, Kool smacked Mecca on the ass before she left out of his place, heading to get her day started with Diamond. Once in the car, Mecca noticed Diamond engaged in a heated conversation, so she decided to sit in silence until she was done. Pulling away from the curb, still on the phone, Mecca noticed Diamond heading south, when the mall was up north. Tapping her on the shoulder, Diamond held up one finger, signaling for her to hold, which Mecca did. The two of them cruised for about another mile before Diamond finally ended her call.

"Damn, hey bitch, how are you?" Mecca sarcastically stated, causing Diamond to bust out laughing.

"My bad bitch, that was Wayne, I hate his ass." Diamond replied, referring to her on and off boyfriend of five years.

According to Diamond, Wayne was the best yet worst thing that ever happened to her. Listening to the horror stories made Mecca appreciate the little drama she had going on since it was nothing compared to Diamond's love life.

"Yall ass crazy but where the fuck you headed, the mall not this way." Mecca pointed out, noticing Diamond had yet changed directions.

"Oh, we going to the mall after breakfast, its Saturday morning." Diamond replied, turning the music up in the truck.

"Ok but breakfast where?" Mecca quizzed, looking at her out the corner of her eye.

"My parents house, we have breakfast every Saturday and…."

"AND BITCH I DID NOT SIGN UP FOR THIS! BREAKFAST AT YO PARENTS HOUSE? TAKE ME BACK HOME!" She yelled, causing Diamond to laugh at her dramatics.

"Girl chill, my family aint gon bite." Diamond chuckled, glancing over at Mecca who still looked upset.

"I aint trying to hear none of that. Why you aint tell me before?"

"Because you would have said no and I aint got time for that." Diamond informed her, still laughing at Mecca's reaction.

"Girl aint shit funny. I can't believe you. I don't know these people." Mecca thought aloud, ready to curse Diamond out even more.

"You know me and Capone and Jaylan. My parents chilled as fuck. Those the only people to know…. Oh and Jaylan's wife Brianna but she's cool too." Diamond replied, making Mecca feel a little better.

Happy that she put thought into her attire, Mecca folded her arms across her chest and remained quiet the rest of the ride. She wasn't mad at Diamond; she just didn't want to face Capone again. The two of them hadn't spoken much since the hospital and that's how Mecca wanted to keep things.

Pulling up to a brick two-story home, Mecca looked around at the manicured grass and fancy cars parked in the driveway. Immediately spotting Capone's jeep, Mecca sucked her teeth as she unbuckled her seatbelt. Getting out of the car, she waited until Diamond was out before heading to the porch.

"This a nice ass crib." She admired aloud as Diamond used her key to enter the home.

Amazed that the inside was just as beautiful as the outside, Mecca followed close behind Diamond as she maneuvered through the home. Stopping in the kitchen first, Mecca stood in the doorway while Diamnd greeted her mother who was at the stove cooking.

"Ma, this my friend Mecca, Mecca this is my mother."

"How you doing Mrs. Brown." Mecca smiled, extending her hand for a handshake.

Mecca watched as Diamond's mother wiped her hands off on the apron she was wearing before reaching for a hug.

"Call me Shannon baby, how are you doing?" she asked, instantly making Mecca feel much more comfortable.

Mecca and their mom shared a hug before she returned back to the food cooking on the stove.

"What you ladies got planned today?" she questioned, taking the biscuits out of the oven.

"Nothing ma, after we leave here, we gon' head to the mall. Mecca birthday coming upppppp!" Diamond sang, grabbing Mecca by the arms, twirling her around in a circle.

Mecca and Ms. Shannon laughed at how excited Diamond was for Mecca's birthday. It reminded her of how Kay acted whenever her birthday was approaching. Feeling down briefly, thinking about her ex best friend, Mecca quickly dismissed those memories and snapped back to reality.

"She so silly." Mecca giggled, pulling away from Diamond who still spun in circles.

"Yes she is but what do you have planned?" Ms. Shannon asked as she began to set the table.

"Here let me help you." Mecca offered, grabbing the stack of plates out of Ms. Shannon's hands.

"Thanks baby." She smiled, now grabbing a few cups out of the cabinet while Mecca placed the plates around the table.

"You're welcome but I'm not really big on birthdays so I probably just chill or study." Mecca finally replied.

"Ma, she so damn lammmmeeeee!" Diamond dramatically yelled, using her fingers to make an "L".

Mecca and Mrs. Shannon shared another laugh at Diamond's expense as she paraded around the kitchen acting silly. The laughs continued for them but stopped for Mecca when Capone and Pip appeared in the doorway.

"What's so -----funny?" he paused, noticing Mecca standing there for the first time.

Mecca wasn't as shocked to see him, seeing how she noticed his car when she pulled up, however, who she was shocked to see was the person standing behind him.

"Oh hey baby, I thought you was still downstairs but I'm just in here clowning with Diamond and Mecca. You hungry?" Ms. Shannon asked her youngest son whose eyes never left off Mecca.

"Yeaaaahhhhh…. I was just about to go on the porch and smoke." He replied, finally breaking stares with Mecca.

"Oh okay. Everything will be done by the time you back." She stated before turning back to the stove, where she resumed cooking.

An awkward silence fell upon the kitchen as Mecca now stared at Pip with nothing but hate in her eyes.

"Damn, if looks could kill." Diamond smirked, elbowing Mecca, getting her attention.

"Yall wanna hit the weed?" Capone asked, raising the already rolled Backwood in the air.

Without hesitation, Diamond walked off, leaving Mecca standing in the middle of the kitchen floor alone.

"Nah, I'm good, I'll finish helping Ms. Shannon." Mecca informed them before cutting her eyes at Pip.

"I'm done baby. Go out there and at least get high off contact. When you done, WE gon finish playing that birthday, okay?" she beamed as she moved around the kitchen.

The sound of Pip smacking her lips could be heard a mile away. Everyone in the room eyes darted to her while she stood there, still staring at Mecca.

"Let me go hit this blunt before I smack this bitch." Mecca said low but not low enough.

Once on the porch, Mecca went down a few steps while Capone, Pip and Diamond stood above her. It was taking everything in Mecca not to snap. She felt like a bitch, knowing she was only a few feet away from the person who killed her little brother and yet, she was playing it cool. She had to stop herself on the strength of Danielle because she promised that she'll allow her to take control.

"Aye friend! I was thinking about throwing a Halloween Party, if I do, who would you come as?" Diamond asked out of the blue, causing Mecca to turn around and frown her face.

"Friend, I have no clue but that's a random ass question." Mecca replied laughing at Diamond's randomness.

Mecca not only shared a birthday with her mother Melissa but with Halloween as well, October 31st. As she explained to Capone's and Diamond's mom, she wasn't big on birthdays, in fact she barely acknowledged hers.

"Aye, if I was to come, I'll dress like my idol." Capone stated while releasing smoke circles in the air.

"IKE TURNER NIGGA!" Diamond yelled causing Mecca to laugh.

"Hell yeah…. I'll be in that bitch like…."

"IKE AND TINA GINA…. IKE AND TINAAAA!" Both Capone and Mecca said in unison, in reference to an old episode of Martin.

The two of them shot each other a look before Capone smiled and winked his eye at her. Completely taking back at his boldness, Mecca played it cool, while Diamond played "Shade Queen."

"Awwww… see that's cute. That little thing yall just did right there." Diamond grinned as she wiggled her finger back and forth between Mecca and Capone.

"Look, imma let yall have yall lil moment, I can't get high anyway." Pip said, walking off, leaving the trio alone.

"BYE BITCH!" Diamond yelled, chucking up the deuces behind her back as she disappeared into the house.

"I gotta piss and I know the food ready." Diamond mumbled before following behind Pip.

Mecca watched as she disappeared as well, leaving her and Capone alone on the cool porch.

"Here!" he said, passing her the blunt.

"You know I don't smoke Capone." She replied, shaking her head no.

"Mannn when you gon' smoke yo first blunt with me?" he asked, walking closer to her as she walked up the stairs.

Mecca paused in motion as she reached for the front door. She turned around slightly, staring into his eyes.

"When yo bitch get her lace front fixed. Capone get the fuck out my face." Mecca snapped, even shocking herself.

She knew the moment those words left her mouth that she had overacted. Not only was she taking out her anger towards Pip on him, she was jealous, seeing her on his arm. Taking Kool up on the offer to move into his crib with him didn't sound so bad after all.

"Look…." He barked, grabbing her hoodie.

Mecca's eyes shifted from his unwanted hand to his eyes as she warned him with her stare to stay away.

"Look, my bad, I aint know you was coming, if I did I would…."

"You would have kept yo bitch at home….. Capone you a clown." Mecca snatched away laughing at the nerve of him.

She proceeds in the house when all of sudden she stopped and turned around to face him again.

"I'll be out yo shit in a week. I'm moving in with Kool." She spoke with intentions on pissing him off the way the same way he had just done her.

"NO THE FUCK YOU AINT!" He barked, the baritone in his voice increasing a few notches.

"I said what I said Capone." She hissed, turning away to leave again when he stopped her for a second.

"Take yo time, as a matter of fact, make sure he move the other bitch out the way before he slide you in." Capone said, brushing passed her and into his parent's house.

"And what the fuck does that supposed to mean?" she quizzed, this time grabbing him by the Nike hoodie he wore.

"I seen ya manz at the gas station with a bitch but I'm sure you already know how the nigga move since you ready to shack up and shit." Capone chuckled, walking away, leaving Mecca standing there, stuck in thought.

Chapter Six

"You good honey?" Mrs. Brown asked Pip as she stormed past the kitchen towards the basement.

Pissed was an understatement. It was no secret to the world that Pip and Capone's sister Diamond didn't get along but inviting Mecca to a family event just to get under her skin was childish. On top of her actions, Capone stayed on the porch even after she left, cracking jokes and shit like everything was cool.

Pip could tell by the way Mecca stared at her that she knew something, which meant that Danielle opened her mouth about Pip's true business adventures. If that was the case, why hadn't Capone approached her about it yet? Did Dani keep the secret to herself or did Mecca have another motive which is why she hadn't said anything to Capone yet?

Pip's mind raced a hundred miles per hour as she tried to figure out what was going on. She couldn't stomach the fact that someone had something to hang over her head and it was little she could do about it.

"You good girl?" Jaylan's wife Bria asked as soon as Pip made it down the basement stairs.

Checking her surroundings, Pip made sure they were alone before she started spazzing out.

"Imma beat Diamond ass." Pip roared, smashing her closed fist into her open hand.

"Girl what now? I'm so sick of you and your sister-in-law." Brianna teased, not realizing how serious the matter actually was.

"No, I'm not playing. Remember I told you about the girl Mecca who seems to be always hanging around?" Pip replied, trying to jog Brianna's memory.

"Anyway, her and Diamond real cool meanwhile I think Capone fucking the lil dirty bitch!" Pip continued but was cut off by Brianna's laughter.

"I'm serious. Shut up and listen. Capone swear they only friends… blah blah blah…. However, I KNOW it's more to it." Pip ranted on while Brianna listened attentively.

"Girl Capone not gon allow nobody, not even his sister, to disrespect you. I honestly feel like it may be innocent. Is he acting weird? Where she at? Where they at? I wanna see what the bitch look like." Brianna rambled on before standing to her feet.

At this point Pip was more worried about Capone finding out about her business than she was about him fucking

Mecca. Mecca wasn't competition and any real man could see that. Sure, she was young and pretty but it took more than looks to be on Pip's level and after she had Capone's baby, Mecca really wouldn't stand a chance.

"They outside on the porch, come on."

Pip and Bri headed upstairs when they heard Mrs. Brown summoned everyone to eat. Detouring from their original plan, the two ladies headed to the kitchen where they took a seat at the table.

"Bae, I saved you a seat here." Pip announced, motioning for Capone to head her way.

Adjusting the empty seat near her, Capone sat down as everyone else pilled in. Pip eyes searched everyone's in the room when a light bulb went off in her head. Smiling to herself, she all of a sudden had an appetite again, which was a good thing since Mrs. Brown was placing the food on the table.

"Everything looks do good MA." Pip complimented as the bowl of hot grits wisped passed her.

"GIRL!" Diamond said aloud, as her eyes rolled in the back of her head.

Pip knew exactly what to say and do to get under Diamond's skin. Understanding that she was too old for games, Pip still played them as long as she had a partner to play with and at that very moment, Mecca and Diamond was pawns in her chest game.

"Hey Daddy, you must of came in through the back." Diamond beamed, standing to her feet as their father and older brother Jaylan entered in the kitchen.

Greeting him with a hug, Pip kept her eyes zoomed in on Diamond just to ensure that she caught all shade thrown her way. If they wanted to play, then let the games begin.

"Daddy, I want you to meet my lil sister Mecca. Mecca this my Pops." Diamond introduced the two just as Mecca stood to her feet.

"Hey Mr. Brown." Mecca greeted him with a friendly hug before sitting back down.

"Mr. Brown is my father. You can call me Dad since Diamond has made you her sister." Redd replied, causing everyone to chuckle expect Pip.

Pip made it known that it was an issue by the way she smacked her lips again, this time even Capone's parent shot her a look. She no longer cared about hiding her emotions, at that point, whatever happened, happened.

After everyone got acquainted, the family began digging into the wonderful meal that was prepared for them. Not only did everything look good, it tasted even better. Pip loved Capone's mom's cooking and although his mom and her mom were close friends, Pip's mother wouldn't be caught dead standing over a stove. Which is probably why she wasn't a fan of cooking.

As Pip stuffed the last piece of bacon in her mouth, she noticed Capone staring at Mecca who seemed not to be paying him any attention. Nudging him hard with her elbow, Capone looked over at her like she lost her mind before cleaning his plate. Pip listened along as Capone parent's held miscellaneous conversations about nothing in particular. Her mind was elsewhere and truthfully, she couldn't wait until breakfast was over so she can handle some business.

"Ma, this was so good!" Diamond stated, standing to her feet, preparing to take her plate to the sink.

"Yeah Ms. Shannon, it was amazing." Mecca chimed in, standing up as well, following behind Diamond.

"Thanks suga but I still aint forgot about the birthday plans…. So what we doing?"" Mrs. Brown asked Mecca, causing Pip to turn up her nose.

Pip always considered her relationship with Capone's parents as a good one. She's known them her whole life, the only grief they every expressed was when her and Capone started dating. With a ten-year age gap, they weren't very happy about it, but they eventually got over it.

"When yo birthday?" Jaylan asked before gulping down the last of the orange juice in his glass.

"October 31st." Mecca replied, returning back to her seat from the garbage.

Pip felt her phone vibrate on the table as the gang engaged in an conversation surrounding Mecca's birthday. Thankful for the distraction, Pip snatched up her phone and read over the text message from Brianna.

Bri: Why the fuck is this Mecca bitch so THICK!? She still aint got shit on you friend ☺

Pip's eyes darted across the table at Brianna who shrugged her shoulders. She must had been looking at Pip while she read her message because her eyes were already glued on her when she looked up. Locking the phone without replying, Pip turned her attention back to the table and waited for everyone to simmer down before she spoke. Grabbing the unused butter knife that was near her, Pip picked up her orange juice glass. striking it three times with the knife, getting everyone's attention. Clearing her throat, she waited until the house was completely quiet before she proceed.

"Capone and I been wrecking our brain trying to find the perfect time to tell everyone but we are expecting."

Pip stood her feet, pushing her chair back, rubbing her semi-flat stomach. Everyone in the room eyes bucked, including Capone. The couple hadn't talked much about the pregnancy which bothered Pip. She assumed that Capone would be just as happy as her about starting a family but she was wrong.

"Oh My God! Are you serious? Why didn't you tell meeeeee." Brianna jumped to her feet excitedly and replied, walking around the table, giving Pip a huge hug.

"Thanks girl. We are so happy." She beamed, cutting her eyes at Mecca who sat there, staring holes into the side of Capone's head.

"WAIT! ARE YOU SERIOUS? WE GON BE GRANDPARENTS!" Mrs. Brown eagerly stated, placing her hand over her heart, still in disbelief.

"Yes ma'am. I can't wait. I hope it's a boy cuz he's going to be a JR." Pip replied, looking down at Capone who still was sitting.

"Congratulations son!"

"Yeah, that's what's up bro."

Redd and Jaylan congratulated him but it was obvious by the look on his face that it was not a celebratory moment for him.

"Diamond, aren't you happy about being an auntie?" Pip looked over in her direction in asked, knowing the answer already.

Diamond shot Pip the look of death before standing to her feet. She slowly fixed the blouse before moving around from the table.

"Mom and Dad, I'm about to head out of here. Jaylan don't forget about the meeting Monday morning at the funeral home. Capone, if I was you, I'll get a DNA test bruh. Let's go friend before I beat the baby out this bitch." Diamond snapped, walking out the front door, leaving everyone with their mouths on the floor.

***

Pip sat in the front seat with her arms folded across her chest as they headed home. She was pissed about the way things went down back at Capone's parents house. She loved the way Shannon and Redd reacted to her pregnancy, she expected Diamond to say some hating shit but what threw her off was, the way Capone was acting.

"All I'm saying is, HAVE MY FUCKING BACK!" she yelled, pounding her fist on the dashboard.

Pip felt Capone looking at her as she ranted on and on about everything that took places moments ago. They left his parents' house without him showing an ounce of happiness about the baby which didn't sit well with her. Pip had gone through so much just to get pregnant even after knowing he didn't want kids. She secretly prayed that his feelings would change when she conceived, now she was hoping that he'll come around, once she started showing.

"If you bang yo fist on my shit again, imma bang yo muthafukn head next." He replied calmly, looking back at the road.

"WHAT THE FUCK IS WRONG WITH YOU!" She screamed, becoming frustrated with the entire situation.

"How you end up pregnant Pip?" he looked over at her again and asked.

"The fuck you mean how? The sperm travels to the egg and…"

"Ava cut it out." Capone interrupted her and said, pulling into the driveway of their home.

"Cut what out. You talking like it's impossible for me to get pregnant. I showed you the test Capone, all three." She replied, unbuckling the seat belt.

"Yeah you showed me A test but that's not what I'm questioning."

"Well what exactly are you questioning nigga?" she jerked her neck in his direction and quizzed.

"Look, all I'm saying is, I pull out, I make sure…."

"PULLING OUT IS NOT AN EFFECTIVE FORM OF BIRTH CONTROL CAPONE. YOU DO KNOW THAT RIGHT!" She yelled, her anger building inside of her as she pieced together what he was saying.

"You trying to say my baby aint yours? You want a test?" she followed up with, calming down a little.

Pip watched Capone let out a long sigh before he took both hands, rubbing them over his waves.

"I gotta take care of some business. You done?" he turned to her and asked, her mouth flying open at the audacity of his comment.

"Fuck you Capone!" she snapped, opening the car door making her exit but not before slamming it shut, actually attempting to shatter the glass.

Pip knew exactly what buttons to press when it came to Capone and since he was pissing her off, she figured that she should return the favor.

Walking off towards the house, Pip pulled her phone out of her purse before turning around to see what Capone was doing. She knew for a fact that he was following close behind her, ready to go to war about slamming his door but to Pip's surprise, he was backing out the driveway, leaving. Quickly going inside her Chanel bag, she searched through the contents inside until she found her phone. Unlocking it with face ID, Pip eagerly searched for Capone's name. After only two rings, the phone went to voicemail, letting her know that he declined the call. She thought about calling him back but instead she went to her contacts and called Danielle. It had almost been a week since she had spoken with her and she couldn't afford for another week to fly by.

"Hello." Dani answered on the fourth ring, which shocked Pip.

The way she had been getting the voicemail lately, she knew for a fact that Dani was intentionally avoiding her, which led her to believe that she had something to hide.

"Damn Young Bull, long time no hear." Pip replied, putting the key inside the front door of her home.

"You been avoiding me like I owe you money." Pip continued, tossing her keys and purse on the couch before flopping down herself.

"You know I broke my phone and on top of all that, my grandfather died. My bad Pip, I been going through it." She replied, making Pip feel a little bad.

"And then on top of all that. I got into it with my sister the night of the party. I've been staying with my friend Stephany since that day." Dani continued as Pip listened on from her spot on the couch.

"What yall get into it for?" Pip quizzed, trying to fill Dani out.

"Stupid shit but fuck that bitch, what up?"

Pip remained quiet as she tried to collect her thoughts and see how things were going to play out. Although Danielle claimed her and her sister was on bad terms, it still didn't mean she hadn't ran her mouth.

"Oh no worries, I understand. Where you at now though? We need to meet up and talk."

Pip waited for a reply from Dani but instead the line went silent.

"HELLO!" she yelled into the phone, pulling it away from her ear to see if the call was connected.

"My bad, my phone fell but that's cool. Where you wanna meet?" Dani stated, causing Pip eyebrow to raise.

"Meet me at Pip's House in two hours, I gotta handle some business first but I'll see you there."

Ending the call, Pip tossed her phone on the side of her before titling her head back, releasing a deep breath. She felt like life was kicking her ass when in fact it should be the other way around. Pip's House was making more money than ever, she was expecting a child, just when things started looking up, a monkey wrench was thrown into the plans. Trying to figure out what to do in regard to Dani and Mecca was stressing her out. Regardless of it all, the Young sisters knew too much and with that being sad, she needed to make arrangements and she knew exactly who to call next.

Chapter Seven

"Damn man, why you aint tell me that you and yo sister got into it?" Nike asked from the passenger seat as Danielle drove him around like a chauffeur.

"Why you so nosey?" Dani snapped, shooting him a look out the corner of her eye.

That was Nike's favorite line whenever Danielle asked him a question, so she mirrored him, seeing how much he liked the response.

"Shorty you wanna be like the kidd so bad. Talking like me and shit. Going to cop the same Timbs as me and shit." He boosted, sitting up in the passenger seat, checking out his reflection in the mirror.

Danielle looked over at him and laughed before focusing back at the road.

"You acting real light skin right now nigga." She chuckled, pulling behind an eighteen-wheeler at the red light.

"But nah for real, why you aint tell me though?" he questioned again, this time in a serious tone.

Dani had no idea that when she lied about being into it with Mecca, Nike would hit her with twenty-one questions about the ordeal. She also answered Pip's call on accident especially since she was in the car with Nike when she called.

"I mean… I don't know. Shit aint a big deal." She finally replied after being unable to elaborate on the lie.

"Look shorty I told you since day one, I aint here to hurt you. I aint even hit yet and you got me talking like a sucker." Nike chuckled shaking his head as he pulled the blunt from behind his ear.

Nike was right, Dani held back when it came to him but how could you blame her? The two of them had been practically joined at the hip as of lately. What they had was more like a friendship, he was the best friend that she always wanted. Recently, Nike had become affectionate with Danielle, completely catching her off guard. He would start off by complimenting her, making her feel all mushy inside, something that no other male had ever done. He would then follow up with little gestures like long hugs whenever they greeted each other. Just a few days ago, Nike pulled her into a kiss, completely shocking her. Although it took her by surprise, she enjoyed it and the two of them hadn't stop locking lips ever since.

"I know Nike, it's just so much more to me than you know." Danielle replied, thinking about how the Dame situation had completely scared her.

He made it damn near impossible for any other member of the male species to get close to her and on top of all that, seeing Dame a few weeks back still plagued her mind.

"Open up to a nigga is all I'm saying Danielle…… DAMN….. shit shouldn't be like pulling teeth." He barked, grabbing his ringing phone out of the cup holder.

Danielle had never been more happy to hear the tone of an Iphone ringer. She had no idea where the conversation was going but at least he was distracted for the time being.

"Wad up sis." He spoke, completely turning down the music.

Danielle immediately recognized the voice on the other end. She wasn't sure why Nike phone was so loud but it was so she listened in.

"Where you at? I got some work for you and I need it done ASAP!" she spoke loudly from the other end.

Making sure to keep her eyes on the road, Danielle did her best to try and act like she wasn't listening.

"I'm on my way to you right now. I was dropping Danielle off anyway. What's up?" he replied, glancing over at Dani and then back out the window.

"Oh so she's in the car with you right now?" Dani heard her ask in a much lower tone, so low that she had to strain to hear.

"Yeaaaaa, what's wrong? Everything good?" he questioned, sitting up straight in the seat.

"Yeah, I'll holler at you when you get here."

Pip ended the call and Nike went back to lighting his blunt like nothing ever happened. Danielle began to wonder what that conversation was about and why did Pip sound so eager in the beginning, but her entire mood changed after finding out she was with Nike. She had even sounded funny when she was on the phone with her. Dani knew her reasoning behind acting strange but now she was beginning to wonder what Pip's problems were.

When they entered the mansion, Nike slapped Danielle on the ass before heading to Pip's office. Dani went the opposite way, up the stairs to find the girls. On the way there, she texted Brandy who let her know that she was already on the estate and that she'll meet her there. Making it to the top of the stairs, she headed straight to Troy's room to check on her first. After knocking twice on the door, Troy's roommate Maria answered before smiling and walking out, leaving the two of them alone.

"Dannniiiii…. Long time no see." Troy jumped up and greeted her with a warm hug.

"Hey girl, I been busy. How you been?" Dani asked, taking a seat on the bed once Troy released her.

Danielle watched as Troy's body language changed. She went from her happy preppy self to looking like she was carrying the world on her shoulders. Taking that as a sign, Dani began to probe a little more.

"Is everything okay? You know you can talk to me about anything." Dani told her, laying it on thick.

Letting out a deep sigh, Troy checked to make sure the door was closed and locked before taking a seat next to Dani on the bed.

"It's my granny. She's really sick and apparently I'm the only one who cares." She paused, rolling her eyes deep in the back of her head before continuing.

"Anyway, he hospital bills are piling up and since all the money is going there, she's about to lose our family home. I seem to be the only one who cares cuz I'm the only person trying to make shit happen. My aunties and uncles don't give a fuck about nobody but themselves, its kinda like, I'm the only one granny can depend on."

Danielle listened as Troy rambled on, spilling all of her family jewels. Troy's family sounded much like Dani's, with her grandmother being their rock too. Thinking long and hard about her next choice of words, Dani took her time and allowed everything to process before she spoke.

"I'm so sorry to hear that but trust and believe, I know exactly how you feel. Is that why you here at Pip's House?" Dani quizzed, turning so she could be faced Troy.

"That is EXACTLY why. I tried stripping but even that money was not fast enough. My cousin Trini told me about this place and here I am." She spoke, tossing her hands in the air before standing to her feet.

Danielle watched Troy move about the room, it was clear that the situation with her grandmother was eating her up.

"What if I could promise you that I could save your granny's house and put way more money in yo pocket than Pip's House ever did."

Troy's neck snapped in the direction of Danielle, staring at her with every word she spoke. Dani could see the wheels spinning in Troy's head as if she had a glass skull. Truthfully, Dani wasn't sure what made her promise such a ridiculous thing however, if everything went as planned, she would be able to make good on that promise.

"Whatever I gotta do, I'm down." Troy excitedly spoke, automatically putting her trust in Danielle, the same way she had done with Pip.

Now that Dani had Troy and her trust, she wondered and worried if she could put that same trust in Troy. From day one, she had been the only one in the house that she instantly bonded with. Troy made Danielle feel welcome when she needed it most, the most she could do is return the favor.

"Troy sit and listen, I gotta share something with you but it CAN NOT leave these four walls." Dani preached, looking around at the walls as if they could actually talk.

"I swear to God you can trust me Dani, what's up?" a concerned look filled Troy's face as she took a seat like requested.

Danielle sighed deeply, pondering hard if she should tell Troy the truth about Pip and her connection to Coby or not. Brandy already knew and Dani felt like that was too much since she didn't trust a soul. If word got back to Pip then everything, she worked so hard for, would be ruined. Realizing that she needed an extra person on the team if the takeover was going to happen, Danielle swallowed her pride and told Troy everything, from top to bottom.

Tears streamed down Troy's face as she listened to Danielle retell the events from the day Coby was hit and killed by the car. Not only did Danielle's words leave Troy speechless and in tears, it left her wanting revenge just as Dani and Mecca did.

Feeling so much better after getting it off her chest, Troy and Danielle sat and talked for another forty-five minutes, when there was a knock on the door.

"You expecting someone?" Danielle turned to Troy and asked as she stood her feet and headed to the door.

"It's me Brandy." She called out loudly from the other end as if she heard them discussing her.

Giving Troy a head nod, she opened the door, greeting Brandy with a warm smile before closing and locking the door again.

"What's up yall?" Brandy said, flopping down on the bed out of breath.

"You good?" Dani asked, noticing how winded she was.

"Yeah I'm good, just ran up the stairs to tell you this and yall know my fat ass out of shape." She huffed and puffed until she was able to get her breathing under control.

Dani laughed out loud as Brandy's tiny ass exaggerated about her weight. She was skinny as a toothpick, minus the hard belly that was beginning to poke out.

"Running for what? What happened?" Danielle finally asked, eager to know what the rush was about.

Brandy eyes connected with Danielle's before she cut them secretly at Troy.

"She's good. I told her everything." Danielle stated, filling her in and letting her know it was ok to continue.

"Ok so bitch listen. Pip knows something. I'm not sure what she know but its something." Brandy advised them, now causing Danielle's wheels in her head to turn.

"Why you say that?" she quizzed calmly, wondering what bought Brandy to this conclusion.

"Listen…. So look right. I been working side by side with her all day. She keep asking me questions about you and shit….."

"Questions like what?" both Dani and Troy asked in unison, briefly looking at each other and then back at Brandy.

"Basically asking what all I knew about you. She asked about some girl name Mecca too." Brandy recalled, giving the girls an ear full.

"That's my sister." Dani mumbled.

"Oh shit! It makes sense then. She think yo sister fucking around with Capone, girl. Pip was talking in circles but from what I gathered from it, she's worried that…."

"Mecca gon tell Capone about this house." Danielle cut her off and stated, shaking her head up and down.

"EXACTLY! The old sneaky ass bitch scared the cat out the bag." Brandy replied, nodding her head as well.

Danielle sat there, drowning in her own thoughts, piecing it all together. She had more shit on Pip, shit that could not only end her career but the relationship with her man.

"I wonder what her next move gon be. "Troy added in from her spot near the door.

"I'm not sure but I played my role so Dani it's best that we still act like we hate each other…"

"Bitch I never hated you…." Dani cut her off and explained.

"Well bitch I hated you, but I don't anymore." Brandy smiled, winking her right eye at Danielle as she laughed.

"Knowing Pip, like I do she's going to move you out the way, simply because you know too much. Exactly how… I have no clue but I'll find out" Brandy continued, finally answering the original question.

"Move me out the way" Danielle repeated Brandy's words over and over in her head.

The shit sounded like a death threat and with Pip's ways, that wouldn't surprise her.

"Aight let me go holler at her before she come looking for me. I'll be in touch." Dani stated, standing to her feet, adjusting the high waist jeans she wore.

Walking towards the door, she still couldn't seem to get Brandy's words out if her head. Was Pip really going to send for her? If so, she had to be ready for whatever whenever she decided to come. Reaching for the doorknob, Danielle paused at the sound of Brandy calling her name.

"Aye Dani, I spoke with the other girls and everybody down but don't worry, I stuck to the plan and didn't say too much. Once we get the big shit out the way, the little shit will follow." She explained, these words sounding like music to her ears.

"Thanks so much. You have no idea how much I appreciate it." She thanked her, meaning every word.

"We doing this for Coby." Troy smiled, reassuring Dani that she too had her back as well.

"Thanks." She rejoiced again before unlocking the door and heading to see Pip.

"Aye G, be careful, this a different type of bitch we dealing with." Brandy warned her one last time before she disappeared down the hall.

Chapter Eight

It had been a week since the disastrous breakfast at Diamond and Capone's parent's house. Tea was spilled left and right, all of it leaving Mecca feeling some type of way. Hearing that Capone and Pip were expecting that first child crushed Mecca, for more reasons than one. Although she'll never admit it out loud, she had feelings for Capone, feelings that magically appeared out of nowhere. Of course, she found him attractive, any woman with eyes could see that, however, her feelings for him was more than physical.

"I'm telling you sister; I don't think that's that mans baby. Pip so damn dirty, I wouldn't be surprised if it was Mac's child or some other random nigga on the streets." Danielle spoke from her side of the couch as her and Mecca shared a blanket in front of the tv.

"And I still can't believe that shit. I feel….I feel even more conflicted than I did before. At first it was just me telling him how his bitch was a murder and pimp, now I gotta find a way to tell this man that she a liar and cheater too." Mecca thought, truly torn about the matter altogether.

"Yea, you in a fucked-up situation, I'll hate to be you." Dani shrugged, not helping out at all.

The way Danielle spoke, you'll think she wasn't in deeper shit, when in fact, she was. Dani and Mecca had been working around the clock trying to execute their plans for Pip. With Danielle having the girls in the brothel on her side, things were starting to look up for them but it was far from over.

"You still not answering that boy calls?" Mecca heard Dani ask, noticing her ignoring Kool's call once again.

"Fuck dude!" Mecca spat, meaning each and every word while she sat up straight.

Watching Danielle do the same, Mecca rolled her eyes, already knowing where the conversation was headed.

"I like Capone, I really do BUT.... Niggas be bitter too sus. Maybe he aint really see Kool with a bitch and you are overacting for nothing." Dani spoke, sliding on her house shoes just as their was a knock on the door.

"You expecting someone?" Mecca asked with a puzzled look on her face.

"Nope but yo birthday IS tomorrow. Maybe it's a telegrammed stripper or some shit." Danielle joked as she headed to answer the door.

Mecca watched as she stood on her tippy toes looking through the peephole. Without speaking through the door to the person on the other end, Dani turned around, displaying a devilish smile before pulling the door open.

"What up Dani?"

"What up Kool!" Danielle smirked, moving to the side allowing him full entrance to the one place that he was not welcomed.

"So you gon keep acting like a little ass kid and not answer my calls or text messages?" Kool addressed Mecca as soon as he entered.

"I aint got shit to say to you." She replied, folding her arms across her chest, not wanting to talk.

It took Mecca three days to address Kool about Capone spotting him at the gas station with an unknown bitch. Of course, Kool denied it, even getting extremely upset at Mecca for asking him about it. After a heated argument that led nowhere, Mecca ended up blocking Kool for two days but unblocked him when she started missing him.

"Like I told you before, buddy ass a hater and imma slap the shit outta him the next time I see him." Kool threatened, looking like he was ready to make promise on that threat.

"Why you wanna slap a muthafucker cuz you wrong and caught up?" Mecca asked, standing to her feet, ready for war.

"I told yo silly ass, I aint cheating on you and I don't even remember what day dude lame ass talking about." He barked, stepping around the couch into her personal space.

"The day I was in the hospital for that asthma attack. You were with some bitch in a black bodysuit." Mecca recalled, thinking back to the conversation with Diamond who got more details from Capone.

Mecca watched as a slight smile appeared on Kool's face before he went inside his pocket and pulled out his phone. Standing there still with her arms folded across her chest, Mecca watched as he placed a Facetime.

"What's up bro?" a woman's soft voice spoke through the speakers.

"Kalenna, when is your birthday?" Kool asked, staring intensely into Mecca's eyes.

"It's October 17th, whyyyyyy?" she curiously sang in the phone.

"That's the day of your asthma attack, right?" Kool removed the phone from in front of his face and asked.

Shaking her head up and down, Mecca waited patiently for him to get to the point.

"What you wear on yo birthday sis?" Kool placed the phone back in front of him and continued to ask.

"Kelvin, what's wrong, you scaring me."

"Kalenna, I'm good, just answer the question." He informed her, letting out a deep breath of frustration.

"A Versace all- black bodysuit. Why?"

"Nothing, that's all……. tell momma I'll be over there in the morning, I love you, bye."

Kool ended the call with her sister, leaving Mecca standing there looking stupid. Grabbing her by her arm, Kool pulled Mecca's stubborn behind towards him, into his arms.

"I feel soooo stupid. I'm sorry baby." She mumbled, burying her embarrassed face inside his big chest.

Mecca did feel bad, when she approached Kool about it, she didn't even give him a chance to explain. She was pissed about that on top of the Capone situation; therefore, she took all of her frustration and anger out on him.

"Mecca, when I told you that I love you, I meant that shit. I aint here to hurt you but…."

"I'm wrong, I'm sorry. You never gave me a reason not to trust you and I apologize for taking another niggas word over yours." She cut him off in mid-sentence and expressed to him.

"Aight but you need to decide what you gon do cuz after I check his bitch ass about running his mouth like a bitch, you really gon have to move." Kool replied, pulling her off of him so he could look her in the eyes.

The last thing she needed was for Kool and Capone to have beef. The two of them were alike in many ways which was extremely dangerous.

"Ok, I'll start getting my things together Monday." Mecca promised him, since Diamond found a Halloween party for them to attend tonight and her birthday was tomorrow.

Kissing Mecca on the forehead, Kool promised to get up with her later after the party so they could bring in her birthday together. Agreeing with him, she got one last hug before he left locking the doors behind him. Mecca retuned back to the living room, turning off the tv, grabbing her phone before bussing in on Danielle.

"WHO YOU ON THE PHONE WITH?" Mecca screamed, purposely trying to frighten her but instead she rolled over, sticking up her middle finger.

"Nike let me call you back." She spoke into the phone before ending the call and giving Mecca her full attention.

Flying onto the bed, Mecca landed directly on top of Danielle, completely smashing her.

"GET YO FAT ASS OFF MEEEEE!!!" She yelled, kicking her feet in the air as Mecca laughed, struggling to get off of her.

"What you got planned for tonight?" Mecca asked, laying on the side of Danielle, playing in her hair.

"Me and Nike gon stay in and watch scary movies, it's supposed to rain tonight." She replied, causing Mecca to smile.

She had never known for her sister to actually show interest in a nigga, she was starting to think she was a carpet muncher.

"What time you leaving tonight?" Danielle followed up and asked, shifting in the bed, facing her big sister.

"Diamond said her friend party starts at ten but she's never on time so we should be leaving about eleven."

Diamond had finally convinced Mecca to engage in some Halloween activity. With Halloween being her favorite holiday, Mecca agreed to dress up and get cute, especially since her ninetieth birthday was the very next day.

"Look, I know I'll be long gone before you leave but make sure you send me a picture of you in that consume, okay!" Dani said, snapping her fingers in a circular motion, causing Mecca to laugh.

Rising to her feet, Mecca smacked Danielle across the ass as she laid on her stomach and ran out of the room. She felt good. Her and Kool was back on good terms, although she still felt silly for acting so childish. She meant what she said about moving out, she just didn't how to tell Danielle that they'll be moving in with Kool.

Laying across her the bed, Mecca grabbed a pillow and placed it under her head, getting comfortable. After snatching up her phone, she scrolled through Facebook, Instagram and Snapchat until there was nothing else to see. Turning on her side, Mecca felt herself dozing off but figured since it was only seven 'o'clock, it was okay.

The sound of her phone ringing awoke her slowly as she struggled to find it within the sheets. Missing Diamond's call but noticing the time, nine-thirty, she jumped up but not before dialing Diamond back.

"BITCH I KNOW YOU NOT SLEEP!" Diamond screamed loud into the phone, almost breaking Mecca's eardrums.

"I was but I'm up now, getting ready." She lied, searching through the top drawer, pulling out a black thong.

"I'M OUTSIDE MECCA!" she yelled again as Mecca ran down the hall to the bathroom.

"I swear I'm sorry friend, I just…."

Mecca was cut off by the loud sound of Diamond's annoying ass laugh. Turning the shower on, she waited until she simmered down before she questioned her.

"I'm just playing girl, I'll be there in thirty minutes." Diamond continued laughing, ending the call in Mecca's face.

Placing the phone on the sink, Mecca undressed and jumped in the hot shower that was waiting on her. After handling her hygiene, Mecca was out, dried and headed to her room within fifteen minutes. Slicking her wet hair in a ponytail to the back, Mecca applied lotion all over her body before going inside the closet. Grabbing the YSL shoe box off of the top shelf, Mecca snatched the black leather bodysuit off of the hanger as well. After ten minutes of struggling into the skintight bodysuit, Mecca placed on the signature "YSL" gold heel stilettoes and walked over to the full mirror.

"DAMN MECCA" she boosted before grabbing her mask and red lip stick off of the dresser.

Placing the black mask over her eyes, Mecca double checked her baby hairs before heading over to her ringing phone.

"Im outside for real for real this time!" Diamond laughed again into the phone, this time Mecca hanging up on her first.

Grabbing the YSL black clutch purse to match her heels, Mecca ran a mental checklist in her head before going downstairs to meet Diamond. Spotting her across the street, Mecca inhaled the fall breeze before shuffling over to the Mercedes Benz.

"BITTTTTTTTCCCHHHHHHH!!!!   CATWOMEN WHO? HALLE BERRY WHO? YOU LOOK AMAZING FRIENDDDDD!" Diamond screamed so loud, turning heads from the people outside walking by.

Tickled and embarrassed, Mecca rushed inside, closing the door as fast as she could.

"Why are you so loud Diamond…. DAMN!" Mecca yelled, yanking the seatbelt across her as Diamond laughed.

"I'm so sorry but Mecca……. You look so fucking dope friend. That bodysuit looks painted on, I told you ass to get the small. You're welcome!" Diamond rambled on, pulling away from the curb, heading towards the party.

The short twenty-minute drive consisted of them catching up, when in reality, they talked every day. Of course,

Capone name was mentioned, causing Mecca to catch an instant attitude.

"All jokes aside Mecca…. When I told my brother he should get a test, I meant that shit." Diamond spoke in a serious tone, which surprised the hell out of Mecca.

Now grant you, Mecca knew for a fact that there was a chance Pip's baby could be Mac's but what bought Diamond to her beliefs.

"Why you say that?" Mecca quizzed as they pulled behind a dark blue Maserati in front of the club.

"I honestly don't have any concrete proof but something about that bitch does not sit right with me. I know Capone knows it but the thing with him, he don't give a fuck, he's more concerned about you." Diamond explained, shifting in her seat to face Mecca who stared at an empty spot on the dashboard.

"Diamond, I need to tell you something." She spoke, her eyes slowly gliding away from the empty spot.

"I know for a fact that…."

BANG! BANG! BANG!

Mecca jumped, grabbing her chest before noticing the valet attendant at Diamond's window.

"Nigga scared the shit outta me too." Diamond laughed, pressing the button, turning off the car.

Mecca hesitantly unbuckled her seatbelt before slowly getting out of the car. Stepping onto the curb, she waited for Diamond before the two of them walked hand and hand inside the club. Surpassing the small line, Mecca began to wonder what type of party it actually was. Diamond seemed to know everyone in the line, disguised in costume and all as she greeted them like some type of star.

"Damn Diamond, put me on to your friend." One dude yelled out, causing Mecca to turn around, looking in his direction.

"Capone will kill the both of us. Let's go!" she grabbed her hand and demanded, pulling Mecca along towards the door.

Once behind the double doors, the loud music that was blasting suddenly stopped.

"Damn, did the DJ have to shit!" Mecca joked as Diamond pushed her forward through a set of curtains.

"SURPRISE!" a crowd of people yelled out as Mecca recognized none of the individuals standing in front of her.

"BITCH WHO PARTY?" she turned around and asked Diamond who had her phone in Mecca's face, recording everything.

"WE GOT THE BIRTHDAY GIRL IN THE HOUSE. YO HAPPY BIRTHDAY MECCA!" a female's voice, similar to Mc Lyte blasted through the speakers as the people in the small setting clapped.

"HAPPY BIRTHDAY SISTER!" Danielle appeared from behind Mecca yelling and jumping up and down.

Mecca became dizzy watching her prance around in a yellow and black plaid blazer and skirt set. Glancing down at her legs, Mecca laughed at the white knee highs she wore accompanied by a pair of all-white ones.

"Imma kill you bitch!" Mecca threatened, pulling Danielle into a hug as the two of them began dancing to the music playing.

"As if!" Dani replied, mocking Cher from her favorite movie "Clueless", hence her Halloween costume.

Completely taken back, Mecca began to surf the crowd, noticing a few more familiar faces. Somehow, someway, Diamond was able to invite all her high school friends. A couple classmates from college and a few people from the hood. The rest of the people were Diamond's family and friends, in addition to the twenty girls that came with Danielle.

Making her way around, Mecca greeted everyone as people admired and complimented her look. The majority of the party was in costume which made everything even much more cooler.

"Shiddddd………if I would've known you was coming as Cat Woman, a nigga woulda came as Brue Wayne instead"

Turning around, Mecca came face to face with Capone who wore all black, with a gold bone chain around his neck.

"Nah, Nino Brown fits you better." Mecca leaned in closely to him and whispered before walking off.

Just as Mecca expected, she didn't make it far before Capone pulled at her arm, yanking her back towards him.

"Look, since you not replying to my messages or calls, I wanted to apologize in person. I had no idea shorty was going to make that announcement but…."

"But you knew she was pregnant prior to that day yet you still aint tell me." Mecca cut him off and stated before snatching away.

"Truthfully, its none of your business BUT since I have so much respect for you, I'm apologizing for how shit played out. Pip's my girl and…."

"And yet you are standing here in my face. Thanks for coming Capone but I'm good." She patted him on the chest and said before completely walking away this time.

More and more guest filled-in and although Mecca knew only half the people, she was glad they came because they made the night even more enjoyable. Sliding out of those heels before the first hour, Mecca danced until she couldn't dance no more. The DJ catalog was crazy, and she made sure to keep a mixture going. In need of a drink, Mecca made her way to the bar where she got a bottle of water. Gulping down the cold drink, Mecca closed her eyes, enjoying the taste when her phone began to vibrate in her hand.

Popping her eyes back open, Mecca noticed Capone staring at her from across the dance floor. Directing her action from him and to her phone, Mecca smiled as Kool's name appeared on the screen. Unlocking the mobile device, Mecca read over the message with a huge smile on her face.

Kool: Come outside.

Mecca: I'm not home bae.

Kool: I know. Come outside

Placing the empty water bottle on the bar, Mecca glided across the dance floor to the front door.

"Where you going?" Diamond stopped her and asked before she made it out.

"Kool outtttssiiiddeeeee...." She yelled, still smiling as she zoomed passed her.

Excusing herself as she bumped into a few people, Mecca rushed out the double doors bare foot. Coming to a complete halt, she froze as Kool stood in front of a brand new all-black Tesla with a huge red bow on the hood. Dressed in a gray Nike jogging suit, Kool walked towards her with a bouquet of red roses in one hand and number balloons in the other, displaying the number nineteen.

"Happy Birthday baby, I love you." He spoke, handing her the keys as well as the roses.

"YASSSSSSSSSS!" Diamond appeared out of nowhere yelling as the party moved from inside to outside.

"I LOVE YOU TOO BABY.... I LOVE YOU TOO!" Mecca screamed jumping up and down in Kool's arms.

"Yo sister told me about the party but considering the circumstances, I stayed clear so wont shit fuck up your day. We gon have our own party in Miami when the semester over until then, go back inside and finish enjoying your night….. oh and that extra key on that chain is to my crib. I'll see you later tonight." Kool explained before placing a kiss on her lips, completely taking her breath away.

"No bae fucked that. I'm going home with you now!" she yelled, running back inside to grab her shoes from the table.

Dipping through the crowd going back in as she did coming out, Mecca reached the table where her belongings were but not before colliding with Capone again.

"I see you about to head out. I just wanted to give you your gift before you did. Happy birthday baby." He spoke, placing a kiss on her forehead and handing her a plain white square box.

Opening the box, Mecca stared at two gold keys.

"Keys? What's these keys to Capone?" she yelled out to him as he began to walk away.

"Yo beauty supply Mecca. Happy birthday!"

Chapter Nine

Capone pulled in the driveway behind Mac's silver Infinite truck and killed the engine. Noticing that the rain wasn't letting up, he jumped out and sprinted to the porch, just as it started to hail. Ringing the doorbell, Capone checked for his pistol while he waited on the damp porch.

"Heyyy Capone, Mac aint tell me you were coming over. Come in." Ashlee answered the door and stated, letting him inside the warm home.

"He in the basement?" Capone asked, giving Ashlee a hug before rubbing her round stomach.

"You know it…. I'm cooking, you hungry?" she yelled out as the two of them went their separate ways.

"I'M GOOD ASH…. THANKS!" he yelled back, heading down the basement stairs where he found Mac laid out on the couch.

Sitting up straight, Mac peeked around the corner when he heard Capone approaching, after noticing it was him, he laid back down and waited for his right-hand man to approach.

"What up nigga. You almost loss yo life popping up down here." He joked, sitting up allowing Capone to have a seat.

"Mannnn yo bitch ass aint gon do shit." He chuckled, popping a squat at the end of the couch.

Looking around, Capone noticed how much redecorating Mac and Ash had done. He assumed it was for the baby, which made sense.

"You look stress G, you good?" Mac asked, standing to his feet stretching.

Capone watched Mac make his way over to the bar where he grabbed two glasses, filling them both with White Hennessey.

"Mannnnnn, a nigga aint stressed but this shit gay as fuck." Capone admitted, ready to finally get things off of his chest.

Capone could have easily gone and vented to his brother Jaylan, but Jay always seemed to be bias when it came to him and Pip's relationship. Seeing how Mac has been around since the beginning, Capone knew that his boy would keep shit one hundred with him, which is exactly what he needed.

"What's gay as fuck?" Mac laughed, walking over to Capone with the double-shot that he prepared.

Taking the glass out of his hands, Capone knocked it back with no hesitation, instantly feeling the burning sensation in his chest.

"Pip pregnant…."

"STOP LYING NIGGA!" Mac turned around and yelled, heading back to the bar with both empty glasses.

"I wish I was." Capone paused, trulu wishing that the pregnancy situation was a bad dream.

"But I thought you wanted kids. A big family and shit." Mac recalled from previous conversations had amongst them.

"Nigga I do….. just not with that bitch."

Mac's eyes grew the size of golf balls, it was obvious that he wasn't used to hearing Capone speak about Pip in that manner, but he meant every word. He loved Pip but was not in love with her and things seemed to have been that way for the past few months.

"Damn nigga, that's deep but what you gon' do?" Mac questioned, finally taking a seat on the couch but not before grabbing the remote control to the tv and game.

"I low key wanna tell her to get rid of it but…."

"DAMN G, YOU WANT SHORTY TO GET AN ABORTION?" He shockingly asked, handing Capone the red game controller.

"I don't think it's my baby and…."

"Nigga, Pip aint cheating on you, you know that. I get not being ready but you know that baby yours….. why you are doubting it?" Mac cut him off and quizzed as Capone began to wonder.

"Me and shorty aint even fucking like that and besides…."

"YOU FUCKING THAT BAD ASS BITCH MECCA, AINT YOU?" Mac interrupted him again, this time with a huge smile on his face.

"Watch yo mouth nigga but nawl." Capone replied low, his dick getting hard at the thought of sex with Mecca.

"To be honest bro, I don't even know what to tell you but I know for a fact that Pip wouldn't cheat on you, sis love you man but if I was no longer feeling Ash, I would probably just stick it out, maybe yall situation will change when the baby arrive." Mac assured him but it went in one ear and out the other.

Having a huge family was always a dream of Capone's, a dream that he once had with Pip but somehow, it quickly faded away. He didn't want to use Mecca's presence in his life as an excuse, but all fingers seemed to point that way.

"What happened with you last night? I thought you was sliding through the Halloween party?" Capone asked, changing the subject with attempts on clearing his mind.

"Ohhhhh, something came up." Mac smirked, keeping it short and sweet and Capone knew exactly what that meant.

"How was it though?" he looked up briefly from the game and asked.

"It was smooth, a lot of people from the hood came through…. It was all love." Capone recapped as he selected his NBA player.

"Word! I seen Diamond post a Tesla on Snapchat. Was that one of shorty's gift?"

"Yeah, her nigga bought her that cheap ass whip." Capone replied, ready to stay clear of that conversation but as he expected, Mac probed more.

"Wait….. so shorty got a nigga who buying her cars and shit and you stressing about her? That pussy gotta be good." Mac laughed, causing Capone to chuckle along with him.

The shit sounded funny but what he was dealing with was not a laughing matter. He had no idea that he would fall for

Mecca the way he had. The night of her party when Kool pulled up with her car, he wanted to go outside and air it out but realistically, he knew it wasn't possible. On top of all that, Mecca had been giving him the cold shoulder ever since Pip spilled the beans about her pregnancy.

Capone's sole purpose for coming over was to talk to Mac and get his outlook on things. Based on the type of man Mac was, Capone knew that he was not capable of providing sound advice, however, he still wanted to hear him out.

"Look, I gotta get up outta here. I'm meeting up with Wayne. I'll holler at you later." Capone announced, standing to feet, tossing the game controller on the table in front of him.

A few more words were spoken amongst the two friends about business before Capone was heading up the stairs.

"I'm gone Ash. See you later." Capone said, slipping past the kitchen and out the front door.

Just as he explained to Mac, Capone headed out west to rap it up with Wayne, Diamond's boyfriend, about a few things. Agreeing to meet with him outside of his job, Capone pulled in front of the 10th District, where he left the car running. Shooting Wayne a text, he waited about four minutes before he walked out wearing his Chicago Police Department uniform.

"Waddup bro." Wayne got inside the car and said, greeting him with a head nod.

"Shit. How's pig life?" Capone teased like he always did.

"How's the criminal life nigga? Any new felonies?" Wayne shot back, causing Capone to laugh aloud.

Outside of Mac, Wayne was Capone's best friend and confidante. Although he met him through Diamond, the two of them shared a bond like real brothers.

"But nah for real nigga. I need a favor, I need you to look into something for me." Capone stated, getting down to the real reason for the visit.

"What's new? What's up?" Wayne asked, double checking to make sure that all devices on him was off.

"So there's this nigga I need info on. Street name is Kool. He be over East. The nigga tall, about....."

"Six foot, drive a Jeep?" Wayne cut him off and asked.

Without verbally replying, Capone shook his head up and down as Wayne ran everything by him.

"The nigga part of the East Gang Mafia, those the niggas that....."

"Be robbing motherfuckers." Capone interrupted him this time and added in.

"Exactly and the Kool nigga is the leader of the gang. We been looking at him and his crew for the past year but they move so smooth, it's hard to build a case on them. Just last week, we expect it was them that hit a Brink's truck downtown on State, them bitches walked away with half a million dollars….. that's easy money for them." Wayne explained in detail as Capone took notes.

"It was a shooting over that way, and I know for a fact his name was all over it as well." Wayne continued, providing Capone with an ear full.

"What's up though? What's to him." Wayne turned to Capone and curiously asked.

Capone explained his connection with Kool in great details, including how Mecca played a part. Unlike with Mac, Wayne paid attention, actively listening as he ran down the entire script.

"Diamond talks about Mecca all the time, from what I hear, she's a dope ass chick." Wayne stated once Capone was done with his storytelling.

"Man, she everything." Capone replied, finding himself smiling just at the thought of her.

"Well imma say this, if things are playing out the way you say they are, I suggest that you be careful and watch your back. If Kool feels the same way you feel about Mecca than the three of yall are in a dangerous triangle. I'll keep an eye out but you may wanna get that nigga before he gets you." Wayne advised and Capone knew exactly what he meant by that.

The two of them spoke more about sports, politics, and eventually their conversation led to Wayne and Diamond's relationship. Capone didn't mind lending a listening ear, but Wayne and Diamond's relationship was complicated, something no one outside of them understood. Listening along, Capone grabbed his phone out of the cupholder, noticing an unread message from Mecca. Lately, it was unlikely for her name to appear on is phone especially since the two of them had been at war.

Mecca: I never got the chance to thank last night. When I came back out, you were gone. Capone, shit is so complicated with us.... Idk where to start. Maybe one day soon, we can meet up and talk but again, thanks so much FRIEND!!

Laughing at the shade she threw at the end, Capone placed the phone back in the cupholder without replying. As bad as he wanted to entertain Mecca, he didn't, he had other shit on his mind, like killing her boyfriend and getting him the fuck out the way.

Chapter Ten

"Come in and close the door." Pip requested as she sat behind the cherry oakwood desk in her office at Pip's House.

For the last few weeks, she had been on pens and needles with what all that was going on around her. It seemed like every time she began to put her plan in motion, something always seemed to stop her.

"What up sis? I been trying to get up with you. Everything cool?" Nike closed the door behind him and asked before planting his ass in the red leather seat in front of his God-Sister.

It was true, Pip and Nike seemed to have been playing phone tag and hide and seek as of the past couple days. Either Pip was busy with work or the two of them never had the perfect time alone to talk. The first day that Pip reached out to Nike, he brought Danielle along with him, however, Pip didn't get a chance to speak to neither of them because her father popped up on the estate. Her father's surprised visit halted all her plans for that day, sending her a few steps back. Each time after that, something else always seemed to spring on them. Pip was just happy that she was free and alone with Nike now to go over everything with him.

"I need you to get rid of somebody for me…. Well two people actually." Pip spoke calmly as if putting out a hit on someone's life was normal.

"Say less. Who?" Nike sat up in his seat and pondered as Pip tapped the pen in her hand on the table.

"Danielle and her sister Mecca."

Pip watched as a confused looked spread across Nike's face. She was aware of the time Nike and Dani had been spending together but she's known Nike since he was in pampers, which trumped any relationship he had with a bitch. Coming to him asking him for a favor this size was normal, Pip used Nike because he was young, reckless and simply didn't give a fuck.

"Cool. When you need it done?" he finally asked after registering the order in his head.

"As soon as possible. I go out of town in a week to New York for Kesha's wedding. I would love for it to be done before I get back. Remember, no bodies should ever surface Nike." She explained, staring the young man deep in his eyes.

Shaking his head up and down Nike rose to his feet, turning to head to the door when he stopped and turned back around.

"Sis you know I stay clear of your business but I gotta know…. Why you wanna pop Dani?" Nike questioned, giving her direct eye contact.

Pip thought about his question and the reason behind it before she spoke. It was never like Nike to question an assignment, but she understood why he wanted answers for this one. Ready to give it to him straight, Pip stood to her feet before walking around to the other side of the desk where she stood only a few steps away from Nike.

"Dani knows too much and that's the best way to put it. I know the two of yall been getting close and I understand if you don't wanna….."

"I just wanted to fuck the bitch first, but I got you." He cut her off and laughed, lightening the mood in the office.

Nike turned around, leaving his back to Pip before disappearing out of her sight. Shaking her head and then scratching her scalp, Pip turned and headed back to her desk where she took a seat but not before grabbing her phone.

She felt so much better, like a fifty-pound weigh had just been lifted off her shoulders. Knowing Nike, Dani and Mecca would be dead before noon tomorrow. Pip also knew that with him already having access to Dani, it would be much easier for him to carry out the task. It was obvious that Dani trusted him, therefore he was already in, which made Pip extremely happy.

Moving along, Pip directed her attention to the phone in her hand, accessing the contacts where she selected Brandy's name. Shooting her a text, Pip reminded her about the lunch date the two of them had at four. Noticing that she had an hour before their meeting, Pip placed another call, this time to Mac.

He had still been M.I.A but as recently as this morning, he texted her out of the blue saying that they needed to talk. Calling him right after receiving the text, Mac failed to answer so Pip was trying her luck again since it was a few hours later.

"Wad up?" his deep voice answered, shocking her so much that she had to pull the phone away from her ear to check and see if she had called the right number.

"You said that you wanted to talk. What about?" she asked, trying to act as if she didn't care about him.

"I do. Where you at?" Mac questioned as Pip slid her red bottoms back on from under her desk.

"I'm at work. What up? You wanna meet at the club or can we discuss this over the phone?" she quizzed, placing the call on speaker.

"Meet me at the club in thirty minutes." Mac replied, ending the call in Pip's ear.

Grabbing her Chanel bag and keys, Pip headed out the office and eventually out of Pip's House, on her way to meet Mac. Traffic was light considering the time of day and seeing how since the restaurant she was meeting Brandy at was a few minutes from Mac's club, Pip knew she was good on time. Hitting the expressway, she was pulling inside the lot in record time. Noticing a car already there, Pip figured it was one of the vendors or someone inquiring about a party therefore she paid it no attention.

Heading to the backdoor like she usually did, Pip pulled it, realizing it was lock before she turned and headed to the front. Doing the same at that door, Pip tugged at it, this time it opened with ease. Walking down the hallway, Pip's heels clicked against the floors as she took slow strides to the back where his office was located.

Upon turning the corner, Pip heard arguing, the main voice belonging to a female. Stopping in her tracks, she listened as Mac and Brandy engaged in a heated conversation that took Pip by surprise.

"Look, you need to calm down and lower your voice." She heard Mac say as she moved a little closer to see if she could lay eyes on them.

The way Mac's office was positioned, and the angle Pip stood, she could see inside without either of them seeing her.

"What you want me to do Mac? You basically telling me that I'm in this by myself so fuck you." Brandy yelled one final time before storming out of the room and colliding with Pip in the hallway.

"Pi—Pip. What you doing here?" Brandy questioned just as Mac appeared behind her, leaving out the office as well.

"I-I came here to holler at Mac about--- about – some shit." She replied nervously, her eyes traveling back and forth between Brandy and Mac.

"What yall two in there arguing about? Everything good?" she continued, trying her best to get the heat off of her.

"Everything good sis." Brandy smiled at her before walking off, leaving the two of them standing alone.

Hearing the backdoor slam, Pip waited a few more seconds, ensuring that the coast was clear before she proceeded.

"I thought you stopped fucking that bitch!" Pip snapped, punching Mac in the chest with all her might.

Laughing at her antics, Mac walked away without saying a word, leaving Pip on his heels.

"I am done fucking with her." He finally replied as he walked through the empty club, heading to the bar.

Staring at his back, Pip thought back to the small part of the conversation she overheard and started there.

"What she mean, she's in this by herself Mac?" Pip asked, seriously wanting to know the answer.

It was true, Pip was the reason behind Brandy's and Mac's relationship but that was before she had her own feelings for him. When she originally hooked the two up, it was because Brandy was always around, so she introduced her to her man's best friend. However, once Pip and Mac started messing around, Pip forbid him for seeing Brandy but apparently, he didn't listen.

"Look man, I aint got time for none of this shit right now. The bitch just told me she was pregnant when I already got a baby on the way." Mac barked, clearly frustrated with it all.

"SHE PREGNANT BY WHO MAC?" Pip yelled, her squeaky voice echoing through the empty establishment.

Pip knew damn well she hadn't heard him correctly but what shocked her even more is the way he said it, like it was nothing.

"I can't fuckin believe you. How could you do this to me?" she cried out, but it didn't seem to faze him.

"How the fuck you gon trip when you carrying Capone's baby… aww yeah, congratulations sis!" Mac chuckled, stocking the bar with new liquor, never giving direct eye contact.

Pip felt her blood beginning to boil, although she was pinning the baby on Capone, she knew for a fact that it belonged to Mac. She had no intentions on ever being with Mac but with the news of him having now THREE kids on the way, she was starting to feel some type of way.

"IT'S YO….. you know what, never mind nigga. Good luck!" Pip said before turning to leave, heading back out the way she came in.

If it wasn't one thing, it was another, however, Brandy being pregnant was the last of her worries. With Brandy being so simple-minded and easily influenced, Pip knew that she could convince her to do anything, including killing her unborn child.

Making it back outside to the November breeze, Pip walked around to her car where she found Brandy chilling on the hood. Letting out a deep breath before rolling her eyes to the back of her head, Pip marched over to her, eager to know what she wanted.

"Look, I know we were supposed to have a lunch date and talk but I don't feel good, my stomach hurt." Brandy stated before Pip could fully approach her.

"It's cool, I feel the same. I'll call you later." She replied, walking passed her and to the driver's side.

It was the truth, the news about the pregnancy had her stomach in a knot and she too had suddenly loss her appetite. Getting inside the car, Pip watched Brandy walk off before snatching her phone out of her purse. With the new information she just received, Pip felt the need to cancel all the upcoming appointments that had for the remainder of the day. Her mind was all over the place and now she was beginning to look forward to her trip to New York.

After dishing out text messages and emails, Pip tossed the phone on the passenger's seat before cranking the car. Looking around at her surroundings, she instantly became agitated and snatched the phone again, this time sending a text to Mac.

Pip: For your information, MY BABY belongs to you too. 3 kids on the way, I hope yo dick fall off but not to worry though, our little secret will remain our little secret BABY DADDY!

Knowing that nine times out of ten Mac wasn't going to text back, Pip secured her phone in the cupholder again before pulling away. Making it to the stop sign at the end of the alley, Pip heard her phone chime, indicating she had a text message. Glancing down, she quickly snatched it up, ready to see what Mac had to say.

Mac: Hey Pip, this Ashlee, Mac left THIS phone at home but I'll be sure to deliver the message

Mac: Oh and congrads!!

Chapter Eleven

"You okay girl, you look pissed?" Stephany asked from across the table before breaking off a piece of garlic bread and tossing it in her mouth.

"Nah, I'm good, just calling Nike again, my bad." Dani apologized, placing the phone face down on the table before picking up the glass of water that was in front of her.

It had been a while since they spent time together and the two of them had a lot of catching up to do. With Stephany working overtime at her new position at the bank and the craziness in Danielle's life, it was no wonder why the best friends had been distant lately.

"So word is, Mecca got a new whip and a beauty supply. WHERE THESE NIGGAS AT SHE FUCKING WITH?" Stephany laughed, causing Danielle to join in on the laughter.

"I know right, the bitch got it made. Two niggas WITH MONEY fighting over her and here I am, can't even get a muthafucker to call me back." Danielle replied, referring to the numerous times that she's called Nike's phone.

It had been a day or so since she last spoke with him which was unusual for him. The two of them usually talked and texted all day if they weren't in each other's presence.

Danielle couldn't help but wonder what was going on and if it was something that she did that caused him to act that way towards her. Nike would reply drily to a text message now and then, so Dani knew he was alive and not in trouble but that's all she knew.

"I can't believe you like this nigga for real. No shade bestie but I was starting to think you was a dike." Steph admitted just as the waitress brought their food to the table.

After thanking her and requesting more ketchup, Danielle directed her attention back to Steph who hadn't wasted anytime digging into her meal.

"I aint no fuckn dike. Why do you and Mecca insist on making me a lesbian?" she asked, reflecting back to a recent conversation she had with her big sister about the same thing.

"I'm just saying, I need to meet this Nike boy. He got my friend blowing up his phone and shit."

Danielle decided to remain quiet and feed her face, all the while trying to collect her thoughts. As good as the food was, she still didn't enjoy it, her mind was racing, and everything was beginning to stress her out.

"I love Red Lobster." Stephany smiled, speaking with her mouth full of food.

"But what's new. Fill me in." she continued, placing two shrimps in her mouth.

"I know who killed Coby." Danielle blurted out without warning, completely shocking Stephany.

"I KNOW YOU FUCKN LYING. WHO?" she yelled, angry filling her eyes from hearing the news.

Dani looked around at the eyes that were on them before continuing her story.

"Pip."

"Pip who? Yo Pip? How Danielle?"

From the top, to bottom, Dani filled her best friend in on the events of her life surrounding Coby. No matter how many times she told the story, she felt the rage building in her with every word spoken.

"Come on, let's go beat this bitch ass." Steph snarled as tears began to stream down her face.

"Girl sit down, it's not that simple, now let me tell you what I have planned." Danielle spilled, the same exact way that she had done with Mecca.

Stephany listened as Danielle rambled on and on, never once interrupting her. Dani prayed that her ideas made it through to her and that she didn't sound like a crazy woman.

"So what do you think?" she asked, once she finished, even allowing Steph a few extra seconds to register everything.

"I think it's fucking genius and if you can pull this off, you'll go down in history as the greatest finesser of all time."

Danielle laughed although she knew Stephany was as serious as a heart attack. She didn't consider what she was doing as finessing, she looked at it as getting revenge.

"Thanks, I guess. Mecca thought I was crazy at first but she eventually got on board"

"Let me help, I know EXACTLY what to do!" Stephany beamed from her seat, causing Danielle to smile at her eagerness.

"How bestie? How you gon help?" she teased, picking up the check off the table.

"You bullshitting but I can help for real. Don't yall have an account at my bank?" Stephany asked her, causing Danielle to ponder.

"Yeahhhhh, all our checks do say Bank of America." She confirmed, also realizing that it had been a while since Pip deposited anything in her account.

"Annnnnd I'm the branch manager, right?" Steph asserted as Danielle shook her head up and down in agreement.

"All I gotta do is get Pip's signature on some Beneficiary Forms and the both of yall signatures on some Power of Attorney documents and BOOM!" she yelled, causing eyes to drift to their table again.

Laughing at her silly antics, Danielle listened closely as she spoke, soaking in those words.

"Now how in the fuck am I supposed to get this bitch to sign some paperwork Stephany?" Danielle contested, realizing that it sounded too good to be true.

"Let me worry about that, I got you." she promised, reaching across the table, touching Danielle's arm.

"I can't man. I just can't. If you get caught, that's FED time and I will never put you in that position." She pointed out, dreading the thought of something happening to her closest friend.

"I'm doing this for Coby whether you want me to or not."

It had been so long since Danielle cried yet she fought back the urge at that very moment. Everyone who was helping out did it on the strength of Coby and that alone warmed her heart.

"Ok so look, when this is over, you gotta quit. I know how much you been talking about moving to Puerto Rico with your family and I promise friend, imma get you there, as soon as this fall through. Flight, car… rent money, I got whatever you need to start over fresh." Dani promised her, causing her to cry for the second time that day.

After paying the check, the two friends made more small talk before they got up and headed to the car. Walking out of the restaurant, Danielle's phone chimed, getting a message from Nike. A huge smile invaded her face as she read over the message in front of her.

Nike: Take this trip with me outta town. We need to spend some time alone.

Holding the phone in her hand, Danielle read over the message four more times, while trying to think of a response.

"Damn, what he say?" Steph asked, catching Dani off guard, noticing the look on her face.

"Huh? Who? What you talking about?" she blushed as she climbed in the passengers side of Steph's red Dodge Charger.

"Huh? Who? What you talking bout? Girl shut the fuck up and tell me what he said?" Stephany mocked her before cranking the engine.

Laughing at her silliness, Dani read over the message from Nike.

"But Imma tell him that I cant." Danielle stated, turning to look out the window.

"And why not? You was just crying back at the table about him not being attentive. Make up yo mind bitch."

"I don't know. I like Nike and all but I know eventually he gon wanna fuck and….."

"AND POP THAT PUSSY FOR A REAL NIGGA!" Stephany yelled, twerking in her seat as they drove down Pulaski.

Laughing again at Stephany, Danielle unlocked her phone, finally replying to his message.

Dani: I got alot of work to do but I'll see

Turning the phone to Stephany, showing her the response, she drastically hit the brakes, bringing the car to a strong stop.

"WORK? DANIELLE NICOLE YOUNG…. WHAT WORK? PIP PAYS YOU TO DO NOTHING FRIEND….

NOT A DAMN THING. So I'm confused as to what work you are referring to?"

Bending over in laugher this time, Dani held her stomach before gaining her composure and responding back.

"I meant my own work, not Pip's shit….. dummy!"

"Whatever, all im saying is…. Let that man show you a good time. I bet this the trip you been dying for. Bitch you better go!" Steph encouraged before turning up Megan Thee Stallion song and rapping along.

Chapter Twelve

The sound of loud hard knocks woke Mecca up out of her sleep. Quickly sitting up, her heart pounded through her chest as she looked around the dark empty room.

BOOM! BOOM! BOOM!

Three more loud knocks could be heard coming from the front door. Removing the covers from her body, Mecca eased out of the bed and headed to the door. Tripping over a few boxes, the neon lights from the microwave caught her eye. It was two-fifteen in the morning and she figured it was Danielle, who forgot her keys once again. Wondering why she simply hadn't called first, Mecca stood on her tippy toes, looking out of the peephole.

"Why the fuck is Capone here at this time of night?" she mumbled to herself as she unlocked the door.

Immediately noticing a weird look on his face, Mecca stood to the side allowing him room to pass by.

"Is everything ok? What's wrong?" she questioned, now closing and locking the door back.

"Dani here with you?" he asked, looking around frowning at the moving boxes.

"No, more than likely she's at Stephany's, why? What happened?" she wondered, looking deep in Capone's eyes.

"Mecca, come here, I need you to sit down." He said, motioning her towards the couch as he cut the light on.

Scared more than ever, Mecca hesitantly glided over to the couch, however, she remained standing. Capone walked over and stood in front of her, grabbing her hands before speaking.

"Man ghee, I don't even know how to tell you this shit but….."

"Tell me what? What's wrong? Where is Danielle?" she panicked, breaking away from Capone, running to her bedroom to retrieve her phone.

Hearing Capone approaching from behind over, she looked over her shoulder briefly at him before dialing Danielle's number. After getting the voicemail after the first try, Mecca began to place another call when Capone stopped her.

"It's not Danielle Mecca, it's Kool."

"Wha—Wat---- What you mean it's Kool. What happened to him Capone?" she asked as tears began to cloud her vision.

"I- I just heard from one of my homies over East that he was killed and……"

"You a lie….. You a lie…. Stop lying Capone." She chuckled, shaking her head from side to side.

"Why would you even play like that?" she continued, looking down at her phone as her hands shook uncontrollably.

"I wish I was baby but I'm not." He sadly replied, towering over her as she called Kool's phone.

"You a lie. My nigga aint neva dead….. You gotta be tweakn ghee." She started to cry as Kool's voicemail answered over and over.

"ANSWER KOOL…. ANSWER THE PHONE BABY!" she sobbed aloud, her legs beginning to shake.

Capone pulled Mecca close to him, allowing her tears to soak his Gucci shirt. The pain, the pain Mecca felt was like no other. It was different from when Madea passed away. It was different from when Coby died. The pain she felt in her heart was indescribable. A pain that she would never forget nor want to feel again.

"What happened Capone. I- I just talked to him." She stuttered, not only trying to get her words together but her thoughts as well.

"I heard he was over East on his bike, sum bout running a light and crashing into an ambulance." Capone regretfully reported to her.

"Niggas out there say he was dead on the spot." He continued delivering the news that broke Mecca's heart into a million pieces.

"Come on man, lay down."

Capone guided Mecca to the bed where she climbed to the middle, getting under the covers. Her blurry eyes watched as Capone slipped out of his shoes, climbing in the bed behind her. Pulling her closer to him, Mecca slid over, laying on his chest again.

"I'm sorry for your loss ma. On God I am." Capone whispered as he held Mecca until she cried herself to sleep.

One Week Later

"You so strong sister. I love you. I swear." Mecca heard Danielle say from door as she stood in the full-length mirror, adjusting the black pencil skirt she wore.

It was the morning she had been dreading for the past seven days. The night Capone broke her heart, Mecca's world changed. No, her and Kool didn't have long history, but they had a bond, a special bond. And regardless of what the calendar said, he had a special place in her heart forever.

"Thanks sister. How I look?" Mecca asked, spinning around, giving Danielle a fashion show.

"You look dope as fuck. Thick as fuck and if I liked hoes, I would want to fuck!" Diamond appeared from Danielle and said, causing all three girls to laugh.

"You stupid man. Yall ready?" Danielle quizzed while both Diamond and Mecca nodded their head up and down.

Leaving out the condo, Mecca held back tears as she walked pass the boxes that still contained some of her belongings. She was supposed to be moving in with Kool, not burying him.

Pulling inside the churches parking lot, Mecca took a deep breath as she looked around the crowd of people. Not only was Kool well-known, he was loved dearly and the turnout at his funeral proved that.

"I'm ready to get this shit over with. Come on yall." Mecca sighed before climbing out of Diamond's car.

Waiting for Danielle to get out the back, Mecca grabbed her sister's hand while Diamond grabbed Mecca's other hand, the trio headed inside to pay their last respects with Kool.

"You talked to his mother?" Dani asked, slowly walking up the churches steps.

"Yep. His sister and grandmother too. They asked me to sit with them, but I told them I was good." She replied, walking through the huge wooden doors, immediately spotting the rose gold casket awaiting ahead.

"You ok?" Dani asked, rubbing the middle of her back.

"Yeah, you ready to do this?" Diamond followed up with as Mecca shook her head up and down.

The motorcycle accident was so bad that Kool had to have a closed casket. When Mecca spoke with his mom, she told her that he was unrecognizable, crushing Mecca even more.

"You wanna go up there?" Dani whispered as they headed down the long aisle.

"Nah, maybe afterwards, let's sit right here." Mecca told her, ushering them to a row in the middle of the church.

Being strong had been the only option Mecca had her whole life. Her short nineteen years on the Earth had been nothing but tragic. To be honest, she was at a point where she didn't know how much more she could take.

After being seated for five minutes, the ushers passed out the obituaries before closing the churches door. The sight of Kool's face on the front of that piece of paper brought about the first tears. Flipping it over, Mecca stared at a collage, coming across a photo of them, taken a few months back.

"May the church say Amen!" the Pastor's deep voice rang through Mecca's ears, her eyes darting to the front of the church where he stood at the podium in a black and gray suit.

Mecca was positive that he said more after that, however, she had completely blanked out. Rocking back and forth, the night she lost her virginity to Kool replayed over and over in her head as more and more tears streamed down her face. Listening to the Pastor's words caused Mecca to cry even harder as other memories of the couple plagued her mind.

"This shit can't be real yall. This not fair." She broke down, dropping her face inside the palm of her hands.

Mecca's cries echoed through the church as people sent Kleenex her way, but it was no use, she was a mess.

"Come on sister. You need some fresh air."

Danielle stood up first, followed by Diamond as both ladies helped Mecca to her feet. Excusing themselves as they passed by everyone, Mecca noticed her breathing began to pick up. Searching through the Chanel bag that

Kool bought her last, Mecca found her asthma pump and took three hard pulls. Feeling instant relief, she headed out the church into the crisp November air with her girls on the side of her.

"You wanna get some air and then go back in?" Diamond asked her friend handing her a dry napkin from out of her Gucci purse.

"Nah, I'm good. I wanna get outta here. Take me home." She sobbed as they headed to the parking lot.

Finally getting her emotions under control, Mecca took deep breaths, controlling her breathing as well. She walked to the car hand and hand with Dani and Diamond, the same way they arrived. In the midst of everything going on, she was happy to have two solid people in her corner, especially when she needed them most.

"Is that…. That is Capone."

Hearing Diamond say his name snapped Mecca out of the small trance she was in. Looking up through her swollen eyes, she spotted Capone leaning on the hood of Diamond's car, waiting for them to arrive.

"Definitely didn't expect to see you here." Diamond said to her brother as all three girls eyed him suspiciously.

Without replying, Capone rose off of the hood and walked towards Mecca, staring deep in her eyes as he headed her way.

"Shorty, I'm here for you." He calmly spoke, his words causing Mecca to melt in his arms.

Crying on his chest in the middle of the parking lot. Mecca listened as Capone whispered in her ear, making promises that she prayed he could keep.

Chapter Thirteen

"When the last time you talked to Mac?" Capone heard Pip yell out from behind the bathroom doors inside their bedroom.

Realizing that was the third time she asked about Mac in two days, Capone began to wonder why she wanted to know so badly.

"Nah, not in a few days. Why?" he yelled back, just as the door opened and out walked Pip wearing nothing but a towel.

"I'm just asking. I haven't talked to Ashlee either, I was just wondering…."

Pip slowly walked over to where Capone was sitting at on the edge of the bed. Stopping in front of him, Pip used her knees to pry open his legs, standing directly in between them. Dropping the towel and exposing her perfect naked body, Pip seductively looked down at Capone, licking her lips.

Looking up at his girlfriend of the past two years, Capone felt absolutely nothing and honestly, he had no idea how things even got to that point. If you asked someone from the outside looking in, they would strongly suggest that

Mecca was reason, but Capone felt in his heart, it was something different than that.

"I got twenty-minutes before Tiff gets here to go shopping. We can do a lot in twenty-minutes." She winked her eye before bending down, placing a kiss on his lips.

"Nah, go handle that. I gotta go holler at my Pops about some shit." Capone informed her before scooting her naked body to the side and standing to his feet.

"YOU GOT ME FUCK'D UP CAPONE!" She screamed out loud, causing him to turn around and look at her like she was crazy.

"Girl, gon' on and get dressed, aint nobody got time for that shit," he replied, dismissing her, leaving her standing in the middle of the floor, ass naked.

Heading down the stairs, Capone went directly out the front door, to his car where he prepared to talk to his father. Over the past week, shit had been hectic, and he needed someone levelheaded and full of wisdom to rap with. He had tried with Mac and even Wayne, but those conversations didn't go well.

Playing the latest Rick Ross album, Port of Miami 2, Capone cruised the streets to his parent's house, with hopes of leaving with more understanding than when he arrived.

Pulling into the driveway thirty minutes later, Capone killed the engine and jumped out.

"What up old man?" Capone said, greeting his father who raked up multi-colored leaves in their front yard.

"Old man? Who the fuck you talking to?" his Dad questioned, placing the rake against the porch, approaching his son with open arms.

Capone's dad pulled him into a manly hug before he continued with his chores while Capone took a seat on the porch steps.

"Where mom?" he asked, looking around, noticing how much his parent's neighborhood had changed.

"She went somewhere with Diamond. What you up to?" Mr. Brown quizzed, taking a seat next his youngest son.

Letting out a deep sigh, Capone wondered where he should start, figuring the top would be best, that's what he did. Capone poured his heart out, revealing everything to his father as far as his love life was concerned. He watched as father listened on, shaking his head up and down, agreeing and disagreeing with what Capone said. After putting everything on the table, he waited for his father to speak but instead he remained mute.

"Do you know the difference between loving someone and being in love with someone son?" Mr. Brown finally spoke, looking ahead at the cars that drove down the block.

"Yeah, I know all about that." Capone advised him, wondering where he was headed.

"Do you love Pip?" he questioned and without having to think twice, Capone answered him.

"Yeah I love shorty. I love her to the point whereas, I wouldn't want anything bad to happen to her." He answered him truthfully, meaning every word.

"What about Mecca. How you feel about her?" Pops followed up with.

"Mannnn, that's my rider Pops. I fucks with Mecca hard…"

"But do you love her?" Mr. Brown cut him off in mid-sentence and asked, turning now to face Capone.

"I do man, I love the shit outta Mecca." He lowered his head and admitted aloud for the first time.

"Ok, you love two women. That aint shit new but let me ask you this. Why do you love Pip Capone?"

With that question, Capone had to stop and ponder before he answered it. He dug deep within, trying to find the most appropriate response but he came up empty.

"I guess with Pip, it's the history shit. She been rocking with me this long and it wasn't until recently whereas I started questioning us."

"Did these questions surface when Mecca came on the scene?" his Dad asked, causing Capone to think back to months ago.

He didn't have to do much thinking, he knew that Mecca was the reason he was slowly drifting away from Pip, that along with Pip's insecurities. Shaking his head up and down, Capone agreed with his father, letting him know that those feelings did happen when Mecca came into the picture.

"I aint trying to hurt nobody but…."

"Hurt comes with love son, it's inevitable, certain shit simply can't be avoided but on the other hand, you gon' fuck around and hurt yourself, trying to keep everyone else happy. From this conversation, I can easily tell that Mecca is where you wanna be and if that is the case, be real with yourself and Pip, you at least owe her that. Don't waste nobody time son." Mr. Brown explained while Capone listened closely, retaining all the knowledge he was distributing.

"Thanks Pops, imma head outta here. Thanks for the talk." He stood to his feet and stated before pulling his father up as well.

Capone laughed as his father grunted, truly showing his age. Colliding for another hug, the two men said their goodbyes before Capone headed to his next destination, with his father's words still ringing through his ears.

After another thirty-minute drive, Capone found himself out west again, this time he was getting off the elevator, heading to his old condo, hoping that Mecca was home. He hadn't took the time to stop off by the garage to see if her car was there, nor did he even bother to call. He needed to see her now and preparing her for his visit was not in the plans.

"What you doing here? Everything okay cuz last time you popped up on me Capone….." she paused, her eyes following him as he entered without a welcome wagon.

"The news you delivered wasn't so good." She continued, a slight smile invading her beautiful face.

Her spirits were high, it was nice seeing that she was in a good mood, especially since it had only been a day since the services. When he showed up at the funeral, he was there solely for Mecca and regardless of how much he respected the dead, it was still fuck that nigga Kool. Capone couldn't believe the niggas luck, he had a price tag on his head and the day before Capone people was set to take him out, he died in the accident. Slightly grateful that things played out that way, Capone knew the guilt of causing Mecca that much pain would eat away at him for the rest of his life.

"I came to talk, no more bad news ma." He informed her, heading inside the kitchen.

"You cook?" he turned to her and asked, standing with the refrigerator wide open.

"I just put some chicken breast and veggies in the oven. Yo bitch really don't feed you huh?" Mecca laughed, causing Capone to chuckle himself.

Mecca was the queen of shade but the little jabs she threw didn't faze Capone at all, in fact, he was ready to see how far she could really throw.

"Nah but I know my new bitch gon' make sure I eat good. Aint that right Mecca?" Capone shot back, laughing at the stunned look on Mecca's face.

"Yo new bitch? Who is that?" she twisted her head around in his direction and questioned, placing her hands on her hips.

Closing the fridge, Capone walked over to where she was standing and grabbed her chin, pulling her face to his.

"YOU! But I know you still mourning and shit so imma take my time." He flirted openly with her for the first time ever.

"I gotta piss, find a movie for us to watch, I'll be back." He ordered, walking down the hall to the bathroom.

After handling his business, Capone washed his hands and returned back to the living room where he found Mecca snuggled up on the couch with the remote control in hand.

"Scoot over." He demanded, pushing her feet aside and taking a seat.

"What we watching?" he quizzed, grabbing her legs and placing them on top of his lap.

Quickly moving her feet away, Capone chuckled at her reaction before grabbing her legs again, doing the same thing as before. The second time around, Mecca stayed put, even getting cozy under her personal blanket.

"You not sharing?" he asked, pulling the pink and tan blanket off of her and onto him.

"You hungry and cold? Nigga you gotta go!" she joked, fixing the blanket so that it was enough to go around.

After starting the movie "Belly", Capone tuned in fully while Mecca seemed to barely watch it.

"What's wrong? You good?" he asked her, noticing that she seemed zoned out, staring at the floor.

"Aw nah, I'm good." She assured him, directing her attention back to DMX and Nas.

Capone knew that Mecca had been through a lot and all he wanted to do was take away all her pain. He wanted to ensure that she never relived her past and that her future from that point on was promising. Thinking back to his father's words again, Capone knew for a fact that it was Mecca who had his heart and the cat and mouse game they had been playing for almost a year needed to come to an end.

"Mecca. We need to talk..." he announced, grabbing the remote control and muting the tv.

He knew that his timing was whack and that she just loss her man, but Capone couldn't allow another moment to go by without letting her know how he felt. In his eyes, if he remained silent then that allowed room for another Kool type ass nigga to move in and take his place. He had missed his beat before but he'll be damn'd if it happened again.

"You right we do but I need to go first." She replied, sitting up straight, turning to face him.

As bad as he wanted to blurt things out and get the shit over with, he allowed her to speak first.

"I just wanna say thank you so much for all you've done for me and Dani. On some real shit Capone, I love you and I gotta be there for you how you've been there for me, so it's only right I be real with you." Mecca spoke, drawing Capone in with each word.

The look of seriousness on Mecca's face made him nervous. Here he was, ready to drop a bomb on her and she was the one with a mouth-full."

"Pip's the devil. Not only did the bitch kill Coby, she's running a brothel and…."

"Wait. Wait. What? Slow down Mecca." Capone requested, trying to ensure that he heard her right.

"YO BITCH A PIMP! YO BITCH RAN OVER COBY!" She yelled, making sure her words reached him this time.

Hearing her crystal clear this go around, Capone tried to register the news Mecca had just delivered but none of it made sense. How the fuck was Pip a pimp and most importantly, what made Mecca think that she was the one who hit her little brother. Requesting that she start from the top, Mecca did, giving Capone the shock of his life.

"So how long yall been knowing this Mecca?" he asked calmly, still trying to connect the pieces to the puzzle.

"A few weeks, I wanted to tell you then but promised Dani that I wouldn't. Capone, the hatred that I hold in my heart for that woman is unmatchable. If it wasn't for Danielle, I would have been told you but that's not even the worse part."

Capone wondered how shit could get any worse than they already were. His entire relationship was a lie, the whole Interior Design company was bullshit, Pip was a liar and clearly not to be trusted.

"What else Mecca?" he ask her, snatching his vibrating phone off the glass table in front of them.

While he waited on Mecca to continue the story, a puzzle look invaded his face as he stared at a message from Ashlee. The message looked to be a screenshot from a conversation between Mac and Pip. Enlarging the photo, Capone felt his blood beginning to boil as he read the detailed descriptions in the text message.

"Pip and Mac fuckin and….."

"And according to this, that aint even my baby." Capone said, cutting her off, showing her the screenshot from Ashlee.

Chapter Fourteen

It was Thanksgiving Day and although Pip's flight was set to land the Saturday after, she bagged an earlier flight, specifically to handle business. After receiving the text message from Ashlee, Pip almost lost her mind. She debated on whether or not if she should give Mac a heads up about what had just gone down but after not answering his phone, she gave up.

Avoiding Capone at all cost, Pip stayed away from home, burying herself with work until she left for New York. The entire time she was away, she only spoke to Capone a handful of times, mostly small talk through text messages. She had her reasons for avoiding him, but she wondered why he had been even more distant lately.

There was no question in her mind that Capone still didn't know about her and Mac because if he did, she wouldn't be breathing right now. She knew that their cover was blown, and it was only a matter of time before Capone found out too. Pip was no fool, she knew that she had to disappear for a while before she disappeared permanently.

Scanning the packed airport parking garage for her car, Pip hit the buttons on the alarm, awaking the beast.

Walking over to her black Porsche, she tossed her luggage in the backseat before getting inside and peeling off.

Heading to her parent's house, Pip needed to grab the keys to one of their apartments in Oak Park. She planned on packing slowly, stashing her belongings there until she was officially ready to move back to New York. She knew no matter how much she wanted this family with Capone, it would never happen now. She also knew moving out abruptly would raise eyebrows and Pip needed at least a week or two to get her shit together.

The entire drive over, Pip wrecked her brain on ways to move Pip's House from Chicago to another state. There was no way in hell she was going to let it go so easily especially after all the hard work she put in to build it. Convincing her girls and staff to move would be a breeze but did Pip really want to deal with the headache that came along with it. She couldn't believe that she had gotten herself into the situation that she was in but now was not the time for regrets.

"Ma, I'll be pulling up in a minute." Pip said, placing a call to her mom, reminding her about the visit.

"We not home, just come down to Redd's house and grab the keys. Everybody been asking about you anyway!" her mom advised her before ending the call in her face.

Fuck.Fuck.Fuck

Pip cursed, repeatedly hitting the steering wheel over and over again. Didn't her mother know she was trying to avoid those people? Why would she be over there now out of all times? Pip thought about calling her back and telling her she'll get it later, but she was already there and the last thing she had to waste was time.

Pulling in front of Capone's parent's house, Pip debated about calling her mother so she could bring the keys out, but she knew she'll have to answer fifty questions had she did. Pulling down the sun visor, she checked her reflection in the mirror before getting out. Noticing that none of Capone's cars was in the driveway, only a brand-new Tesla, Pip wondered who car that belonged to before heading across the lawn to the porch. Ringing the doorbell, Pip waited a few seconds before Redd answered the door.

"Heyyyy Pip! Happy Thanksgiving." He greeted her with a half hug before closing the door behind her.

"We just ate but the food is still out. Make you a plate. Everybody in the living room talking." Capone's father explained, leading Pip to where everyone else was.

Loud laughter could be heard as she approached the family inside the living room. Turning the corner, Pip spotted Capone and Diamond on the two-seater while Jaylan, Brianna and Mecca shared the larger sectional. An instant attitude came over her as she watched everyone having the time of their life while she was struggling, putting hers back together.

"Heyyy frrieeennnddd!" Brianna sang, noticing Pip first.

Bria stood to her feet, walking over to Pip with open arms. Pip noticed the look on both Diamond and Mecca's face, but she ignored them.

"What's up baby? How was the wedding?" Capone stood up and questioned, he too grabbing Pip, pulling her into a hug.

"New—New York was good. The wedding was beautiful, Greg said he wish you would have come but I told him that you had to work." Pip replied, soaking in the Gucci cologne that Capone wore, completely taken back by his embrace.

"Is my parent's downstairs in the basement?" she asked, pulling away from him and looking down at her phone.

"Yeah, they down there." Jaylan answered her from his spot on the couch.

Turning to leave, Pip headed to the basement where she found her mother and father, drinking with Capone's parents. After talking to them for about ten minutes, Pip grabbed the keys from her mom and headed back upstairs to leave. She was starving like Marvin but rather die of starvation than stay over there another minute. Pip couldn't stunt, she was nervous and the fact that so many of her secrets were being exposed, had her running around like a chicken with their head cut off. She needed to vent and get some solid advice she so turned to the one person who she knew she could trust, Tiff.

"Damn you leaving so soon?" Brianna yelled out as Pip tried to sneak by them.

"Yeah, I got a headache and that layover got me tired. I'll call you later." She stopped and stood in the foyer and replied.

"Cool, I'll ride with you to the crib and make sure you good." Capone stood to his feet and said, causing Pip's eyes to buck.

"It's cool baby. I'm stopping by Tiffany's house first. I'll see you later." She advised him, walking away before he could object.

You would have thought Pip had fire under her ass, the way she jumped in her car and pulled away. Driving the streets like a bat out of hell, Pip prayed that she caught Tiff before she left and headed to her parent's house. Speeding down her block, Pip slammed on the breaks once she made it in front. Spotting Tiff's car, she silently prayed that she was in there and hadn't jumped in the car with her husband.

"Answer bitch. Answer." Pip panicked, laying it heavy on the doorbell.

Turning around, double checking her surroundings, Pip looked up and down the block, feeling paranoid.

"Bitch I hope you in the labor the way you ringing my bell." Tiff snarled from behind her.

"Oh my God, you here. I need to talk." Pip urgently replied, pushing passed Tiffany, entering her home.

Pip looked around, making sure they were alone before pouring it out all to her best friend. Tiff was the only person who knew about her fucking Mac. As much as Tiff warned Pip, she never listened and now things were coming back, biting her in the ass.

"Wait Ava, so you telling me that you know for a fact that the baby you carrying belongs to Mac and not Capone." A stunned Tiffany asked, trying to recap what she just heard.

"That's exactly what I'm saying but I figured I could get away with it especially since no one knew about me and Mac." Pip answered her, pacing back and forth in the living room.

"And tell me again what the message said from Ashlee?" Tiff requested as Pip pulled up the evidence in her phone, shoving it in her face.

Reading under her breath, Pip watched as she mouthed every word, her mouth dropping to the floor after reading Ashlee's reply.

"Capone gon fucking kill you." Tiffany turned to her friend and stated with a serious look on her face.

"I know Tiff, that's why I'm here. It's just a matter of time before he finds out…. hell, I'm surprised he don't know already." Pip thought aloud, hoping her best friend had answers.

"Have you heard from Ash?"

"Hell no….what that bitch calling me for?" Pip snapped as if Tiff asked her an odd question.

"Don't get mad at me, I'm just trying to help…. Fuck." Tiff spat, walking away from Pip, entering the kitchen.

"I'm so sorry friend, I'm just scared and on top of this, Capone STILL aint said shit to me about Pip's House YET, he still hanging with that lil hoe Mecca." Pip apologized before continuing her story.

"Maybe just maybe, he don't know. What if the Mecca don't know? You sitting here stressing yo self out for nothing BUT, what I will tell you is….. You need to move around ASAP! There's nothing or no one that can stop Capone from hurting you, not even yo Daddy." Tiffany advised, giving Pip and ear full.

Tiff was right, Pip knew she had fucked up big time this time and if she wanted her and her baby to make it, she had to get away from Capone.

"I'm going to pack up some of my things after I leave here. Imma grab me a room for the next two weeks or what not and I'll just tell Capone I'm out of town and…."

"And if you run into him in the streets then what?" Tiff cut her off and asked.

"Then the nigga with me better kill him. I aint no fool, imma have men looking out for me. I just need to lay low until I decide what imma do at Pip's House."

"Can't one of yo girls run it while you make the transition?" Tiff asked her, untwisting a bottle of water.

"Nah…. I mean Brandy but…."

"BRANDY! RIGHT! I like her, have her do it." Tiff eagerly volunteered Brandy's services.

Pip let out a long sigh before leaning against the island bar in the middle of the kitchen. Brandy would be the ideal person for the job. On top of her being around the longest, Pip knew she could trust Brandy with her life.

"I just found out that she got a baby on the way by Mac too." Pip sadly reported, lowering her head.

"That nigga just shooting up the club huh? Yall need to go get checked." Tiff fumed, rolling her eyes in disgust.

As bad as Pip wanted to curse her out, she knew she right, Mac was out there laying it on thick.

"So, yeah that's why I'm unsure about her." Pip replied getting back on topic.

"Does she know about you being pregnant by Mac?" Tiff asked.

"No."

"So, then you sound silly. You have an issue with her, not the other way around, Brandy has absolutely no reason to cross you. I think she's the only person who can do the job"

Again, Tiffany was right, Pip knew Brandy loved her dirty draws so why not take advantage of that bond? She made a mental note to call Brandy and have them meet up and talk as soon as possible. If she planned on slipping away undetected, Brandy would be the only person who could help.

Chapter Fifteen

Pulling into Walmart's parking lot, Danielle double checked for her debit card and ID before getting out of Mecca's Tesla. As bad as she wanted to be in bed, mother nature made a surprise visit, halting all her plans. Breaking the news to Nike that they had to reschedule their weekend getaway went easier than she thought it would. Danielle had been looking forward to spending time with him although she dreaded the sexual awkwardness that came along with it.

Nike was beyond attractive, everything about him turned her on, but she simply wasn't ready for sex yet. Never once having that conversation with him, Danielle knew there was no way for him to know, especially since she always seemed to shut him out.

Trying to stay focus and not grabbed any unnecessary things, Danielle headed straight to the aisle that contained the feminine care products, grabbed what she needed and headed to the register. Spotting a short line, she damn-near ran to it, placing her Always pads on the empty belt.

"I'm closed after you." A young girl with red and blonde hair said to her, causing the woman ahead in line to turn around.

"Ms—Ms--- Miss Peaches?" Danielle stuttered, squinting her eyes trying to see if it fact it was her or not.

"Oh my God…. It's the Young Sister. How you doing baby?" Ms. Peaches smiled, pulling Danielle into a motherly hug.

"You look sooooo good girl. How have you been?" Miss Peaches continued, noticing the change in Danielle's appearance since the last time they seen each other.

"I've been good. Blessed nonetheless." Danielle smiled, still not believing it was her.

"I been looking for you and your sister. How is Mecca?" Nurse Peaches asked, surprising Danielle that she even remembered their names.

"Mecca is great. We just celebrated her birthday… oh and she's the brand-new owner of a beauty supply." Dani beamed, excited to deliver the good news about her sister.

"Shuuuttt up. A new beauty supply. Where at?" Ms. Peaches asked.

"It's still just a store space near Roosevelt and Pulaski. She's literally building it from the ground up." Danielle reported, grabbing the receipt from the cashier.

Stepping off to the side, Dani and Miss Peaches talked for fifteen more minutes, trying to catch up the best way they could.

"I tell you what. I'm cooking tonight celebrating my daughter's promotion. How about you and Mecca come over. Take my number and put it in your phone."

Doing as she requested, Danielle stored the number before promising her that, her and Mecca would be on time. After a few more hugs, Dani was walking out of Walmart, feeling better than she's felt in a long time.

***

"She still look the same Dani? How did you even recognize her?" Mecca asked her from the driver seat as they prepared to head to Miss Peaches house for dinner.

"Yes, she actually look good. Looks a little smaller but other than that, she's still looks the same." Danielle recalled, going through her text messages to retrieve the address Ms. Peaches sent.

Reading it off to Mecca as she typed it into the GPS in her phone, the two sisters headed to catch up with an old friend. Silence fell amongst the car as both sisters seemed to be in their own world. Danielle mostly thinking about

Nike, while she was unsure of what Mecca had on her mind.

"You talked to Pip?" Mecca asked, as if she was reading her thoughts.

"Just short and brief phone conversations. Brandy told me that she texted her this morning saying how she need to talk, and it was urgent. I'm just waiting to hear what she has to say." Danielle replied, looking out the window as they passed by their old neighborhood.

"Oh yeah? Capone said something about her being out of town. I told you how weird she was acting when she popped up at his parent's house. That bitch was in and outta there." Mecca laughed reflecting back on the other day.

"That's crazy….. He a strong nigga, being around her knowing the shit he knows but still playing his role."

"I explained it to him the exact way you explained it to me. I'm just not sure how long he gon be able to hold it in. Capone act like the shit not bothering him but I know he love that bitch, so he has to feel some type pf way."

Danielle was shocked when she found out that Capone agreed to go along with the flow of things, just as everyone else did. However, the pressure was on her to deliver.

Danielle had made so many promises that there was no way she could fuck up now.

"He said they haven't really been around each other. She was out of town and he's been….."

"Sleeping on our couch…yeahhh about that." Danielle interrupted and said.

"Well bitch, technically, that IS his house and…."

"Oh, I'm not complaining about him being there. I'm just confused why he's not sleeping in your bed." Danielle teased, followed by loud giggles that seemed to annoy Mecca.

"Anyway, we need to hurry up and make some moves because…"

"I got this Mecca. You gotta trust me but in the meantime, pay attention, you just passed the house."

Pulling over to the curb, Mecca parked the car before the two of them got out.

"It's that red brick house there." Danielle pointed down the street to the home equipped with Christmas decorations.

Their Uggs crunching under the hard white snow, Danielle and Mecca walked side by side down to the little red house with the black gate around it.

"You'll think Ms. Peaches had small children the way her crib is decorated." Danielle said, admiring the beautiful festive decorations.

"Grandkids probably." Mecca replied before ordering Danielle to ring the bell.

Doing as she was told, the two sisters waited in the cold for someone to answer but they never did.

"Damn do it work?" Mecca barked, ringing the bell again, this time three or four times.

"DANG! I'M COMING!" A small child's voice could be heard from the other side, causing Mecca and Danielle to look at each other.

"Why that sound like….."

"YANAAAAAA!!!"

Danielle and Mecca screamed at the top of their lungs as tears unknowing poured from their eyes. Dropping both of their purses to the ground, Danielle beat Mecca to Yana, picking her up and hugging her.

"Give her here!….Give her here!" Mecca panicked, her hands shaking uncontrollably as she reached for Yana.

Practically snatching her out of Danielle's hands, Mecca held her little sister tight, whispering in her ear that she'll never let her go. Overpowered by emotions, both Danielle and Mecca shielded Yana as the three of them cried.

"I'm happy to see that y'all enjoying y'all surprise." Danielle heard Miss Peaches say through the sniffles and sneezes.

"But how- - - how did you? Like how you?" Dani stuttered, her eyes darting back and forth between Ms. Peaches and Yana.

"I know yall aint think I was gon let this baby sit in DCSF custody. I made some calls and let's just say I know people in high places…..and speaking of high places……there she go!"

Everyone in the room turned to the backdoor where in walked an older woman, who looked to be in her forties. Just from a quick glance, you could tell she was Miss. Peaches daughter, their resemblances were scary.

"I'm back ma, they aint have the bread you wanted so I got….."

Silence fell upon the them as everyone stared at each other oddly, causing the woman to break her train of thought.

"Lena LOOK! These my sisters I've been telling you about." Yana beamed, speaking for the first time since being reunited.

"Mecca and Danielle… Heyyyyy yall. I'm Lena, Debbie's daughter. Nice to finally meet yall." She walked over and spoke before dropping the bags off at the table.

"Nice to meet you too" the both of them said in unison as Lena gave out hugs.

"My mother has been looking for yall like crazy. She called me crying from Walmart parking lot after running into you Danielle. We been looking for yall for almost a year." Lena explained as everyone slowly shifted to the dining room.

"Well when our house caught on fire, we moved in with my friend but ended up having to move from there. Now we live in a condo downtown right off Michigan Avenue." Mecca spilled, filling them in on a small part of their adventurous life.

"Connnnddddoooooooo" Yana replied, stretching her words like the infamous Souljah Boy meme.

Everyone shared a laugh at Yana's expense while Danielle still couldn't believe she was sitting next to her baby sister. Yana had gotten so big over the past months, even growing breast.

"Is that a training bra Yana?" Danielle teased, causing Yana to jump on top of her.

Sharing that moment with her was everything. Danielle often dreamed about how their reunion would turnout, but never in a million years did she expect this.

"That's ok Yana. Danielle just mad cuz she still wear one too." Mecca chimed in laughing, pulling Yana off of Danielle and onto her lap.

"Ohhhh so that's who Yana get her shady ways from?" Lena laughed, pointing at Mecca who smiled from ear to ear.

Everyone sat around and talked until the food was ready. There was so much catching up they had to do but Dani didn't complain, she was happy knowing that Yana was safe and sound. After taking their seats at the table, the conversation continued as they fed their faces. Danielle and Mecca learned that Lena was a Federal Judge, actually one of the first black women in her circuit, which was the cause for the celebratory dinner. Miss Peaches spoke so highly of her daughter, obviously proud of her accomplishments.

"Mecca, what you in school for again?" Lena asked before placing a fork full of string beans in her mouth.

"Business and Finances." She replied, taking a sip from the Pepsi in her cup.

"Good choice. My husband….my bad, ex husband majored in business before turning to politics." Lena stated as three wrinkles in her forehead formed.

"Speaking of that bastard, when was the last time you talked to him?" Ms. Peaches asked Lena, who from the look on her face did not want to talk about it.

"I haven't spoken to him since the last divorce hearing ma." she advised her before getting up from the table and going to the refrigerator.

Walking back over to the table, Ms. Peaches continued to curse out Lena's husband as if he was there to hear it.

"Ma, there's no need to get your blood pressure up. I refuse to walk away with nothing when I helped him become the man he is now." Lena calmly spoke, while Ms. Peaches on the other hand was about to have a heart attack.

"That's the thing. He's a dirty dog and we just have to prove it." Ms. Peaches fumed from her seat at the table as the Young sisters listened on.

"Every dog has its day ma but…."

"But Patrick Summers is a different type of dog." Ms. Peaches hissed, not allowing her daughter to get a word in.

The name Patrick Summers stuck out like a sore thumb inside Danielle's mind. Although the name was common, she was pretty sure she knew it from somewhere personal, unfortunately she couldn't remember where. And then it her.

"I know her husband." Danielle whispered lowly to Mecca, nudging her with her elbow.

"I'm sure you do. Probably heard his name on the news or something." Mecca dismissed her, tuning back into Lena and Ms. Peaches conversation.

"Noooo bitch. He's a gold member at Pip's House." Danielle explained low, still trying to control her voice.

"Ummm yeah, I'm not following you….but hush up so I can hear them." Mecca said, annoyingly waving her off.

"A Gold Member is a high-end client. He's a regular…. BITCH HER HUSBAND FUCKING PROSTUITES AT PIP'S HOUSE!!" Danielle yelled, causing everyone eyes to land on her.

Chapter Sixteen

Capone pulled in front of a two-flat brick building on the westside in Garfield Park before killing the engine. Double checking the address from his message, Capone sent a text before getting out of the car. Making sure his piece was in place, he headed towards the building and up the stairs when the door open.

"What up Capone?" Ashlee's soft voice greeted him before he made it up the stairs.

"What up Ashlee? How you holding up?" he replied, greeting her with a hug before they entered the house, escaping the cold.

"You getting big. How the baby doing?" Capone asked as he stood in the middle of the floor, unsure if he should sit or not.

"The baby good, he getting…."

"HE? Oh so it's a boy? That's dope. I can't wait to have my little mans out here on the basketball court like….."

"Capone how are you holding up? We really haven't talked much since I sent you the message. You've been checking on me day in and day out but, how are you doing?" Ashlee cut him off and asked, making him realize the reason he asked to meet up and talk to her.

"On sum real shit Ash, I'm good. Its crazy cuz I trusted the both of them but other than that, I'm straight but I needed to talk to you before I made my next move." Capone explained, still standing in the same spot.

"Ok cool, come in and sit down. Excuse the mess but my sister's kids a headache. They shit everywhere." Ashlee fused as she removed dolls and toy cars out of the way, offering him a seat.

"I'm good. I aint gon hold you long." Capone advised her as she wobbled around the room trying to organize things.

"Ashlee, you know I love you like a sister but that nigga you pregnant by…."

"I don't care. Do what you gotta do Capone. I already know how the game go and…."

"And with that nigga dead, you and the baby gon be straight. I meant what I said about being there for you. I'm still lil manz God-Daddy." Capone spoke, rubbing Ashlee's belly.

"As long as I'm alive, yall gon be good…. Even when a nigga dead and gone…You and the baby gon' be well taken care of. But outta respect and love for you, I had to let you know what was about to go down." Capone explained as Ashlee nodded her head up and down.

"I know you in the process of planning the shower, let me know what you need, and I'll get everything." He continued as tears began to slide down Ashlee cheeks.

Seeing her cry tugged at Capone's heart. No pregnant woman should be going through the things she was going through. This should be a celebratory moment yet here she was, preparing to be a single mother.

"I love you sis, everything gon be good." He promised before pulling her into a hug.

They made small talk for another ten minutes before Capone was heading out the door.

"Thanks so much for everything Capone!" Ashlee yelled out as he headed down the stairs.

"You good Ash, hit my phone if you need me." He yelled back before hitting the locks on his car.

"OH AND CAPONE!" Ash yelled out again, causing him to turn around in the middle of the street.

"What about Pip? That bitch need her ass beat." She stated, causing him to laugh aloud.

"Go get some rest Ash, I got this." Capone informed her before getting inside and peeling away.

Making it to the expressway, Capone grabbed his phone to call Pip. He hadn't spoken with her since she's been supposedly out of town and he still needed to play his role.

"What's up beautiful? How's New York?" he asked as soon as the call connected.

"Hey- - Hi- - Hey baby. I'm good, just left the spa with Kesh, heading back to her crib now. What's up?" she lied as Capone listened on.

He wanted to blow her cover so bad but knew that now was not the time. After finally sitting down and talking to Danielle about Pip's House, Capone understood where she was coming from. There was so much to gain and what better way to hurt a person than taking everything away from them.

"She's about to get in the car so we can go to the mall right now…."

"But I thought you just said yall was headed to….. nevermind baby. Call me later." Capone requested before ending the call in Pinocchio's face.

Chuckling to himself, Capone shook his head at the woman who he once loved. After all Pip's secrets were revealed, Capone started noticing things that he let slide before such as the money. He would joke with Pip all the time about how much money she made, even saying she must sell pussy. Pip had so many opportunities to come forward and tell the truth, but she never did. Honestly, Capone could have gotten over her business with the brothel, truthfully, he thought it was genius, it was simply the way she went about things that he didn't like.

Turning the music up to take his mind off of Pip's and her shenanigans, Capone did eighty in a fifty-five zone as he headed to his next destination when the sound of his phone ringing blared through his speakers, interrupting the smooth tunes of Drake. Looking at the dash, noticing it was Mecca calling, Capone quickly answered the call.

"Yo" he said into the phone, making a right onto to Diamond's block.

"I'm headed to the grocery store, you want something?" Mecca asked causing a huge smile to creep upon Capone's face.

"I'm good man…."

"As a matter of fact, grab me some Frosted Flakes, some Flamin Hots annnndddd a Ginger-Ale." Capone replied, running down his grocery list to her.

Her laughter blaring through the speakers, Mecca promised to grab everything he requested before ending the call. Getting out the car, Capone headed to the front door but when he reached for the knob, the door was yanked opened.

"Damn, what's yo problem?" he asked Diamond who stood in front of him with the look of death on her face.

"How much time you think I'll get for killing a cop?" she asked, turning around looking back inside the house before directing her attention back to her brother.

"Look, I just came to talk to Wayne and…."

"Man you aint gotta explain shit to her crazy ass, come in bruh." Wayne appeared in the doorway and said, causing Capone's eyes to shift back and forth between the couple.

"Aye nigga should I come back later?" Capone told him, ready to turn around and head back to his car.

Diamond and Wayne were the modern-day Ethel and Fred. Although they loved each other to death, the two of them fought like cats and dogs. Being a brother, Capone would usually be opposed to disrespect towards his sister, but he knew Wayne and trusted him to never hurt her. On top of being on their payroll, Wayne was his brother, more than a member on the team.

"My muthafuckn brother aint gotta come back." Diamond cursed, twisting her fingers and neck in Wayne's face.

"GIRL SHUT THEEEEEEE FUCK UP! COME IN CAPONE!" Wayne barked, walking inside leaving Diamond alone on the porch, arguing with herself.

Still laughing at Mr. and Mrs. Smith, Capone entered the apartment the two shared for a few years. Heading directly to the kitchen, Capone went inside on of the cabinets where he found a brand-new box of fruit snacks.

"Nigga don't come over here eating our shit."

"I thought we left yo ass on the porch." Wayne replied, as Capone peeled open the bag, placing a hand-full in his mouth.

"Yall the only couple who stay strapped with snacks like yall got kids." He replied, walking away into the living room, leaving them alone in the kitchen.

Before taking a seat on their burnt orange sectional, Capone grabbed the remote control, turning on the huge flat screen on their wall. Listening as they argued, Capone flipped through the guide, settling on the news. After a few segments about violence around the city, the odd couple returned back, smiling and laughing like nothing happened.

"Aight well I'm headed to check on the restaurant, see you bruh." Diamond smile at Capone before turning around, giving Wayne a peck on the lips.

Amazed at how bipolar their relationship was, Capone decided to remain quiet and get down to business.

"I need a favor." he blurted at, the moment he heard the front door close.

"I already guess that nigga, what up?" Wayne replied, taking a seat on the other end of the couch.

"It's a small favor compared to the other shit I ask you for." Capone advised him, being truthful and serious.

Noticing that Wayne seemed to be listening along, Capone continued and explained the reason for the visit.

"I noticed the other day when I was riding down 16th and Trumbull that there's cameras on the poles. They been there long?"

"Yeahhh…ummm a few years. Why? What up?"

"Can you get some footage pulled if I give you an exact date and time." Capone asked him, unsure if that was possible or not.

"Yeah, in about an hour or so. Won't take long at all." He assured him, reaching inside his pocket retrieving his phone.

"Looking for anything specific?" Wayne quizzed, pausing briefly and looking over at him.

"Yeah....Just a vehicle and license plates. I wanna report a hit and run murder."

Chapter Seventeen

"Girl they almost made me catch a case over some Ranch dressing." Brandy fussed, handing Pip both drinks before closing the door.

Pip walked ahead of Brandy over to the small sitting area inside the hotel room she had been calling home for the past few days. So far, her laying low had been going well. According to the world, excluding Tiffany and Brandy, she was in New York, helping her cousin out. Something deep within Pip's spirit told her that something wasn't right. On top of Danielle's distantness, she hadn't heard from Mac since the last time she saw him at the club. Ashlee deactivated all of her social sites and Capone seemed to catch an attitude every time Mac's name was mentioned.

"I need some wine with these wings." Brandy said, standing to her feet heading towards the kitchen area.

"Pour me a glass." Pip requested, digging inside the Wing Stop bag, stealing a fry.

"Herrreee you go." Brandy said, handing Pip the cup since they didn't have wine glasses in the room.

"Thank you girl but should you be drinking….I mean with the baby and all." Pip said, opening up Pandora's box.

Neither of the ladies had spoken about what Pip overheard at the club but she needed to know she could trust Brandy, therefore, they had to start with the elephant in room.

"I got rid of the baby Wednesday, that's why I aint answer your call all that day." Brandy informed her, hanging her head low.

"Wow. I'm sorry to hear that." Pip lied, trying to mask the happiness on her face.

"Nah. Nah. It's cool. I aint trying to be a single parent anyway." Brandy replied, cutting her eyes at Pip, making her feel some type of way.

Maybe she shouldn't have taken it personal, after all like Tiffany said, it's not like Brandy knows she's carrying Mac's baby. The issue lied with her and not the other way around.

"So, you sounded a little worried over the phone. Is everything good?" Brandy asked, snapping Pip out of the light trance she was in.

"Huh?.....Oh, my bad but yeah…. I aint wanna do this over the phone." Pip paused, taking a huge gulp from the red wine Brandy had given her.

Assuming she drunk it too fast, Pip felt dizzy for a moment, but it quickly wore off. Placing the cup back down, she continued the conversation with Brandy.

"A lot is about to change; I'm making a transition to Washington D.C…."

"WASHINGTON D.C" Brandy blurted out, just as Pip expected.

"Hear me out. Although Chicago has been good to us, the DMV will treat us much better. Now this is going to be a quick and sudden move, I need…."

"How sudden?" Brandy interrupted and questioned with a raised eyebrow.

Any other time, Pip would become frustrated with all the questions. Under any other circumstances, she would have reminded her who the boss was and asked her nicely to shut the fuck up. But realizing that you can catch more bees with honey than shit, Pip remained calm and answered all her questions.

"I'm booking me a flight tonight for in about two days. I got a few more loose ends to tie up and then, I'm gone."

Brandy sat in silence and Pip understood that it took time to register it all, so she stayed patient. An unsure looked leaked from her facial expression but there was no room for doubt.

"Although I'll be away. You'll be here getting the girl ready for the move. Everything will take a few months but while I'm over in D.C building, you'll be running all daily function here."

"And Capone gon be with….."

"DON'T TELL A SOUL ABOUT THIS BRANDY, NOT EVEN CAPONE. ESPEICALLY NOT CAPONE!" she spoke with some much passion in her voice, she knew Brandy had to feel her.

"Ummm…ummm ok." a confused Brandy replied as Pip took another sip from her wine.

Feeling a little buzzed, Pip stood to her feet and headed to the garbage to throw the food away. Returning back to the sitting area, she grabbed her phone and flopped down.

"You talked to Mac?" Pip asked, clearly catching Brandy off guard.

"Nope, not in about two days." She recalled, rolling her eyes to the back of her head.

Laughing aloud, although she was really pissed off at the fact that she's spoken to him more recently than she had. Pip tried to play with off with a fake smile.

"Yeah, seems that none of us has. I hope he ok." she replied soberly, becoming a bit worried herself.

It was one thing for Mac to ignore her but for no one close to have spoken with him, was a little weird.

"Yeah, I'm glad you feel that way cuz I don't care. Now back to this move. When you leaving again?" Brandy asked, changing the subject.

"Oh girl, that reminds me…."

Pip stood to her feet and went over to her purse where she pulled out her MacBook Pro. Walking back over to Brandy, she placed the laptop on the wooden coffee table in front of them and opened it up.

"I need to book my flight before I be stuck with some bullshit ass Spirit." Pip cringed, thinking about that horrific flight she took a few years ago.

"What about a place? You staying at a hotel down there?" Brandy pried as Pip went to Southwest to book her flight.

"Nope. I got a relator who has the perfect spot for me. I've done a virtual tour, e-signed some paperwork and now all I gotta do is move in. Once my living situation is in order, then I'll start looking for a new home for my girls."

"Damn, you got it all planned out huh?" Brandy chuckled as Pip typed away on the keyboard.

"Yup! And now my flight is booked….. on some real shit Brandy, I'm looking forward to starting over fresh." Pip boosted, thinking about how even after everything that happened, she was granted a second chance.

Silence fell upon the hotel room as both ladies entertained the many thoughts circuiting in their heads. Pip was starting to feel better about the entire situation, when just days ago, she was stressed and on the verge of suicide. Everything was starting to fall in place, and she loved it. Although she was losing her life in Chicago, including Capone, she still had her baby and D.C was the Stepdaddy capital.

"How about you email me your flight itinerary and your new address in Washington." Brandy suggested, just as Pip began to feel lightheaded again.

"Ok I'll do it now." Pip replied, shaking her head side to side.

"You ok? You don't look so good." Brandy replied with a nervous look in her eyes.

"I'm straight just a little dizzy but I just sent that email."

"I think I need to lay down." Pip continued, grabbing her vibrating phone before walking over to the bed.

Out of nowhere, Pip felt ill, almost positive that it was the food, she pulled her hair in a ponytail before getting in the bed. Blaming it on the meal and the baby, she just wanted to go to sleep but for some reason, her phone kept vibrating. Remembering that she just tossed it on the bed, she lazily looked through the covers until she found it.

"You okay?" Pip heard Brandy yell from the living room.

"I'm good!" she yelled back, unlocking the phone, staring down at the message on her screen.

It felt like time stopped and the world stopped spinning for Pip as she couldn't believe her eyes.

"You smiling hard as fuck. Care to share?" Brandy appeared out of nowhere and asked, catching Pip in a happy moment.

"Oh…oh… just more good news." She replied, glancing up at Brandy and then back at the message from her Godbrother.

Nike: I got Dani with me now. About to handle that!

Chapter Eighteen

Danielle slept the entire two hour drive to Wisconsin, while Nike controlled the wheel, getting them there safe. On top of her period being off and finding Yana, Dani figured why not take Nike up on his offer for a quick getaway. This was her first time she's been away alone with a boy and she was starting to feel awkward already. Danielle knew all her issues and insecurities stemmed from Dame and regardless of how hard she tried not to take it out on Nike, she still did.

During the ride over, Dani noticed him texting a lot, making her wonder if it was another female who had his attention. She was pretty sure that it was some bitch prettier than her who was fucking and sucking him good.

"The bedroom back here." Nike said as they entered this cozy cabin in a wooded area a few miles from the city.

"How did you find this place? It's beautiful" Dani said admiring the old school cabin set up, resembling the ones in those scary movies.

"Ahh—one of my homies told me about this lil low key spot." Nike advised her, dropping their bags on the King size bed in the Master bedroom.

"Ohhh, so you bring all yo bitches here huh?" she semi-joked, rolling her eyes and folding her arms across her chest.

Dani watched as Nike looked over at her, shaking his head before walking over towards her.

"Chill ma, you the only bitch I bring here." He joked, causing Danielle to punch him in the chest with a closed fist.

"Ahhhh….nnahhhh… I'm just playing shorty…. Come here."

Nike pulled Danielle into a bear hug while she twisted and turned, trying to loosen his grip. Allowing her to break loose just a little, Nike began kissing her on the neck, making her melt at his touch. Loving the feeling of his lips on her neck a little too much, Danielle pushed him away, sending him tumbling a few steps back. Without saying a word, the two of them stared at each other intensively, as if they were reading the other's mind.

"You know what Dani…."

"FUCK IT!" Nike barked, throwing his hands in the air, walking away.

Danielle allowed him to leave the room, giving herself time to get her thoughts together. She understood Nike being frustrated, he was a horny young man but what she didn't like was, him making her feel like she's in the wrong for feeling the way she felt.

"So that's why we came here, so you can fuck?" Danielle stormed into the living room and asked, catching Nike sitting on the couch on his phone.

"I could fuck back at the crib." He replied nonchalantly, never once looking up from his phone.

Wanting to curse his rude ass out so badly, Danielle decided not to, instead she took a solo tour of the cabin. Trying to clear her mind as she did the walk-through, Danielle debated on whether or not she should make Nike take her home. She loved the time they spent together but no matter how hard she tried, she couldn't break out of her shell.

"You done being stupid?"

Turning around from staring out the window, Dani frowned at Nike who stood in the doorway, rolling a blunt.

"You rude ass fuck. Boy fuck you." She snapped, pushing passed him but only making it a few feet before he grabbed her.

"Let me go and take me home." She roared as Nike remained as cool as a summer breeze.

"I'm not taking you no where. We finna smoke this blunt and talk. Come on." He said, grabbing her by the hand, leading her to the couch.

No matter how many times Dani told Nike that she didn't smoke, he still offered the blunt to her and today would be no different. After drying the blunt, the two of them sat in silence as Nike took three hard pulls before handing the it to Danielle. With no explanation for her reflexes, Dani took the blunt from him before hitting it, immediately coughing.

"Slow down Big Dog." Nike laughed, patting her back as she coughed up a lung.

"Let's try it again, this time a little smoother." He coached as she followed his instructions, getting better results the second time around.

Instantly feeling the effects of the weed, Danielle began to smile for no reason.

"Don't start that tweakn shit Dani." Nike warned, taking the blunt away from her and hitting it again.

The two of them silently kept the blunt in rotation, Dani enjoying her second high experience a little too much. Starting to reflect on old memories, Danielle laughed to herself as she thought back to the time when Yana told Madea that Dani and Mecca were smoking weed but it was a Black-n-Mild. Madea went crazy, damn near having a heart attack for no reason at all.

"What's so funny?" Nike asked her as he began to roll another blunt.

"I was just thinking about my little sister Yana." She confessed, now smiling thinking about the last time she saw her.

Since being reunited, both Dani and Mecca have been to see Yana every single day. Miss Peaches agreed to allow her to spend her two-week Christmas break with her sisters and all three of them were excited about that.

"Your little sister. You don't talk about her often, why?" Nike quizzed, making Danielle realize that he was right. She had shared little to nothing with him about her past life.

"Her name Yana and we just found her; she was in DCSF custody." She confessed again, the weed making her open up.

"Oh word. Why?" Nike asked, prying a little too much now for Dani's liking.

She had never sat down and told a soul about her life and the people that knew about it only knew because they were there to witness it. Dani cared about Nike, but she now felt herself falling for him, something that she didn't like at all.

"Why you so shield man, I aint trying to hurt…."

Nike paused as if he caught himself from saying something that he shouldn't' be saying.

"Look, all I'm saying is…. Holding that shit in aint good especially when you got a muthafucker that'll listen, but I'm gone from it."

Danielle could tell by the look on his face that he had given up for real this time. Although she was still unsure about whether or not she should open up, Dani took some time to weigh her options. Holding everything in was killing her and especially as of lately, since running into Dame.

"I got a rough life. Can we keep it as that?" she asked him, feeling like she said enough already.

"Tell me something that I don't know Danielle. I'm asking what's to you? Why you so scared?" he looked deep in her eyes and asked, pulling at the strings on her heart.

"Nike…. Nike… I -I- I simply can't. You wont understand." She stuttered, hoping he'll get the picture and leave it alone.

"Nah man, you gotta talk to me. Let's start off with, how you know Pip?" Nike asked her, reaching out with his arms, pulling her closer to him.

It was that touch again that made her tense up, but why? Why when Nike wasn't the reason she was hurting, Dame was.

"I was raped." Dani blurted out, releasing a deep breath when she was done.

"RAPED BY WHO? WHO THE FUCK TOUCHED YOU?" He jumped up and yelled, his yellow skin instantly turning red.

"Calm down Nike. Calm down." She softly spoke, slowly pulling him back down on the couch.

After a few moments of silence and several deep breaths, Nike proceeded to grill Danielle.

"Who touched you and when?" he calmly asked this time, causing Danielle to smile.

"It was my mother's boyfriend."

Danielle let go of the hurt and spoke from the heart as she told Nike the gruel details of her past, holding nothing back. Although she saw the hurt on his face, he never not once opened his mouth and interrupted her. The nightmare about Dame led Dani to telling him about Pip saving her from the abortion ass whooping she got. After dropping story after story, Danielle paused when it was time to talk about Coby. Taking a deep breath, she relived the worst day of her life, fighting back tears as she spoke.

"Aight that's enough. Come here." Nike said, wrapping his arms around Danielle as she cried for the first time in forever.

It felt good letting it out and although Nike was the last person she thought she'll ever vent to, she didn't regret choosing him.

"No more hurting man and I put that on my life Danielle." Nike whispered in her ear as she continued to soak up his shirt.

He allowed her to cry until she felt like she was done, never once letting her go. Just from that gesture alone, Danielle felt closer to him. She knew he was a genuine nigga.

"Aye bae, they ever find out who hit your little brother?" Dani heard Nike ask, her eyes popping wide open.

Danielle knew this is where the problem lies, the connection amongst her, Pip and Nike. Figuring that she had already told him a lot, there was no need to start lying now.

"Remember the night we went to the strip club? Well, I ran into Brandy in the back room, shorty was drunk as fuck and she got to saying….."

Danielle felt like Dr. Seuss, the way she was doing all that storytelling. She also felt like a huge weight was lifted off of her shoulders, which was most important.

"Pause shorty, so you telling me that Pip hit him?" Nike cut her off for the first time and asked, while Danielle shook her head up and down slowly.

"Ohhhh soooo that's why that bitch want you dead?" he mumbled under his breath, but Danielle heard him loud and clear.

"COME AGAIN? YOU SAY WHAT?" she bucked up and asked, leaving Nike still sitting, trying to piece things together.

"Listen to me. I only rented this cabin for a night but imma holler at the manager to get it longer….."

"Nike I can't stay here, I got shit to do…" she cut him off and said, now standing to her feet to face him.

"Just shut the fuck up and listen…..You gon stay here and out of the way until I figure this shit out."

"FIGURE WHAT OUT?" She shouted as loud as she could.

"Pip sent me to kill you so…. "

"So you bought me here to kill me nigga?" Danielle asked, slowly backing away like they did killers in scary movies.

"Bring yo silly ass back here." He laughed but she still had yet to hear anything funny.

"I did not bring you hear to kill you. I came here to see what was going on. On some real shit Dani, I love you and although I knew I wasn't going to kill you then, I know who imma have to kill now." Nike grunted, walking over to the table, getting his phone.

"Aye be quiet." He told her, just as the phone began to ring on speaker.

"God-Bruh, what's good?" Pip's groggy voice sounded through the phone.

"It's done."

"Ohhhhhh…….. ITS done, huh?" Pip repeated, her voice sounding much more upbeat than before.

"Yep, the bitch DEAD." Nike turned to Danielle and said.

Chapter Nineteen

Mecca stuffed the last piece of her sausage biscuit in her mouth before turning off her car and getting out. She had ridden past this same shopping center a million times, but this was the first time she's been there as a business owner. CBS – "Coby's Beauty Supply," was smack dab in the middle of the hood and Mecca wouldn't have had it any other way. Outside of always wanting to be a business owner, Mecca specifically wanted it in the hood, a place where she could relate to her customers and bring some positive revenue to her community.

Sorting through the three keys on her key chain, Mecca selected the one for the front door and proceeded pass the nail shop, over to the vacant storefront.

"Me-Mecca, is that you?"

Turning around, Mecca searched for the person calling her name but didn't see a soul behind her.

"Mecca, that is you."

Following the voice again, Mecca's eyes landed across the parking lot where Kayla was waving dramatically. The last time the ex-best friends had spoken was when Kay put Mecca out after her brother Darrius tried raping her.

"Girl, I ain't even recognize you. How you been?" Kay jogged from across the parking lot and asked as if they were on the best of terms.

"I - I- I'm good. I'm blessed nonetheless, how you been?" she asked, giving her a full look from head to toe.

Kayla looked the exact same, minus the huge seven months belly she carried around with her. Not surprised at all by her pregnancy, Mecca stared at her former best friend with a blank expression on her face.

"What? You coming to get your nails done?" Kay asked, looking Mecca up and down.

"Mecca, you look amazing, you really do. Actually, it was Jay who noticed your car, I just wasn't expecting YOU to get out of it." She laughed at the shade she threw as if Mecca didn't catch it.

"You done Kay?" Mecca asked with an attitude because honestly, she was over the small talk.

"Dammmmnnnnnn…. Don't do that Mecca. I always wanted to apologize for what happened with you and Darrius. I should have had your back, but I was scared….he was my brother and…"

"And you thought it was cool for him to go around raping motherfuckers." Mecca cut her off and stated, leaving her with a dumb look on her face.

"NO! I did not feel that that's why I just…."

"It was nice seeing you Kayla, but I got work to do." Mecca interrupted her again, this time completely dismissing her and walking off.

"WORK? You work in this strip mall?" Kay yelled out, obviously not taking the hint.

Inserting her key inside the door, Mecca ignored Kayla but heard her footsteps rapidly approaching.

"Wait, I'm lost." Kay walked up on the side of Mecca and stated, looking along as she gained access to the vacant store.

"This my store Kay and…."

"OH MY FUCKING GOD! YOU FINALLY GOT YOUR BEAUTY SUPPLY!" Kayla excitedly yelled, causing random bystanders to look their way.

Mecca thought about the long nights the two of them used to stay up and talk about their dreams. She always talked about her many businesses, while Kay's dreams consisted of her being a basketball wife, living in a carefree world.

"I'm happy at least one of our dreams have come true." Kay lowered her head and said in a somber tone.

Awkwardness floated around them as both women searched for words to say. Mecca knew that one day she'd run into Kay, she just didn't know how that moment would go or how she would react.

"My bad for being late, I had to handle something over East."

Capone's deep voice interrupted their train of thought as they still stood outside the store. Neither one of them noticed him approaching, and the shocked look on their faces told it all.

"Capone?" Kayla twisted her head to the side, squinting her eyes as if it helped her see better.

"What up!" he glanced over at her and spoke before directing his attention back to Mecca.

"How long you been out here and why yo phone keeps going to voicemail?" he quizzed from his spot on the sidewalk.

"It's dead on the charger right now. I thought you were coming back over last night, what happened?" she asked him.

"I fell asleep on the couch and…."

"Wait? Yall together, together?" Kay asked, jumping in their conversation without invitation.

"Kay, is there anything else I can help with cuz if not...."

"Say no more Mecca. I get the picture. I just came over here to say that I'm sorry for everything and that you look gorgeous. I wish you nothing but the best in life."

And with that said, Kay was headed back across the street, leaving Mecca and Capone alone.

"How that happen?" Capone asked, pointing behind him at Kay as Mecca finally unlocked the doors to her store.

"She saw me when I was getting out the car and...... OH MY GOD.....THIS PLACE IS HUGE!"

Mecca's eyes lit up like a Christmas tree as she scanned the store that belonged to her, her decorative skills going into full mode.

"Imma put the cash register here. The weave on the back wall, oh, and I'm only selling black products by black entrepreneurs. Imma have security right here cuz I'll be damn'd if these people fuck up my shit."

Mecca rambled on and on while Capone listened, laughed, and encouraged her. He had been by her side, day in and day out, spending most of his nights either on the couch or in his old bedroom. Everyone in her life was helping her cope with Kool's death, and although she still missed him like crazy, she was in a good space in life.

"You talked to your girlfriend? I ain't heard her name being mentioned in a while." Mecca spoke as she headed to the back of the store to check out the office and storage space.

"You steady trying to be funny and shit. That ain't my bitch, you are." Capone replied, causing Mecca to laugh.

She purposely did that only because she knew it would get under his skin and on top of that, he made her feel all mushy inside whenever he referred to her as his woman.

"She wants me to think she's in New York but ain't no telling where that bitch at," Capone replied, joining her in the empty office.

"Wellllll, I spoke with Danielle this morning, and according to Brandy, Pip is staying at a hotel in Aurora. That crazy-ass woman got a whole escape plan ready and in motion." Mecca explained to him as she cut off the bathroom lights exiting the back area.

"On top of all that, Pip emailed Brandy all her flight info and the address and shit to her new crib." Mecca continued, cutting off the remainder of the lights in the store.

"So this bitch think she El Chapo huh?" Capone chuckled to himself, following close behind Mecca, his eyes glued to her ass.

"I don't know who the bitch think she is, but she got the Young sisters fucked up. Turns out, her flight leaves in two days and she has no plans whatsoever on coming back. She's shutting some parts of the operation down, but because she loves money so much, she's going to have Brandy doing everything from here."

Mecca continued to fill Capone in on everything that was going on. He, on the other hand, had been rather quiet when it came to the whole ordeal. She knew that he too had to have a lot on his mind, but unlike the women around him, he didn't show it.

"Look, you don't worry about shit. I got you Mecca. You focus on building your brand and allow the universe to handle Pip." He assured her one last time before the two of them went their separate ways.

Chapter Twenty

Danielle waited outside of Yana's school amongst the other parents dressed in an oversized black hoodie, a pair of dark shades, her hair pulled to the back in a ponytail, with a black skully on top. Looking around occasionally, Dani waited impatiently for her little sister to be released. Just as the thought left her mind, Yana came walking out, talking to two other girls her age. Spotting each other at the same time, both Dani and Yana smiled before Yana took off running towards her.

"How was school big head?" Danielle asked her as soon as Yana, and her two long pigtails reached her.

"LIT! You know today was the last day right….. so we had a pizza party, and they let us listen to music. We even watched *Lean On Me*….."

"*Lean On Me*? Why was yall watching *Lean On Me* Yana?" Danielle asked, stopping at the crosswalk, grabbing Yana's hand.

"I don't know, but it was good." She shrugged, getting inside the car as Dani held the door open for her.

Walking around to the other side, Danielle looked both ways three times before getting inside the heated seats of Mecca's car. Taking off towards Miss Peaches house,

Danielle made it to the light before Yana started her bullshit.

"Why you dressed like that?"

"Dress like what Yana?" Dani cut her eyes at her little sister and asked, trying to see what her aim was.

"Dressed like you in Witness Protection." She replied, hinting to Danielle and how she was fully covered in forty-degree weather.

Unable to hold in it, Dani burst out in laughter, laughing so hard that she missed her turn. No, she wasn't in Witness Protection, but she was supposed to be dead, at least according to Pip. To be perfectly honest, Danielle wasn't surprised that Pip put a price on her head. Now, what did surprise her was who she asked to do it.

Not only did Dani come clean the night at the cabin, so did Nike. He explained the relationship between him and her. Dani also found out that Nike did most, if not all of Pip's dirty work. And just as Danielle had expected, Pip wasn't shit without her foot soldiers. Too bad for her, because those same foot soldiers were now Dani's riders.

"Just mind yo business and get out the car before I beat yo ass." Danielle threatened, quickly getting out the car, chasing her up the street.

Yana ran off at top speed up the sidewalk, ducking and dodging the ice like it was nothing while Dani took her time, ensuring that she didn't slip and fall. As expected, Yana made it to Miss Peaches house before she did, and by the time she did, Danielle was out of breath.

"Yo- - Yo – Ass cheated." Dani bent over and fussed, her throat burning, her eyes watering.

There was no way in the world, a soon-to-be eighteen-year-old should be out of shape the way she was. Dani made a mental note to get a gym membership as soon as all the drama was dead.

"Come on girl, you only ran down five houses." Yana teased, ringing the doorbell has Danielle struggled up the stairs. Just as she made it to the top landing, Miss Peaches was opening the front door, welcoming them inside.

"Dani, you ok? I ain't know it was that damn cold out there." Miss Peaches looked her up and down and said, causing Yana to scream out in laughter.

"I TOLD YOUUUUU." Yana sang, heading down the hall to her room to pack her bags.

Just as planned, Yana was staying with Danielle and Mecca the two weeks she was out of school on Christmas break. After leaving there, they were going to pick up

Mecca, and the three of them were going Christmas tree shopping. Spending the holidays with her sisters and not having to stress about money and gifts was a blessing. A blessing that Danielle never expected to see.

"I thought that was Lena's car out there, where she at?" Dani asked, looking behind her and out the window.

"She's in the bathroom downstairs, she should be up any minute now."

"Who should be up any minute now?" Lena appeared from behind and asked, causing both Dani and Miss Peaches to laugh.

"Speaking of the devil." The two of them said in unison as Lena and Dani hugged before they both took a seat.

The ladies sat around and talked while Yana packed in her bedroom. Speaking mostly about the holidays and how they expected to spend them. Danielle had never been excited about Christmas like she was now. Just as the conversation about gifts started, Yana magically appeared from her room, ready to go.

"Oh no ladies. Don't stop talking on account of little ole me. Just act like I'm not here." she walked by, waving her small hands in the air, taking a seat on the couch.

Sharing a laugh with everyone else, Danielle stood to her feet, checking to make sure nothing fell out her pockets, before heading to the door.

"I'll see yall later. Come on girl."

Grabbing Yana's overnight bag off the floor, the two sisters headed towards the front door with Miss Peaches and Lena behind them.

"Ok, yall drive safe, and Yana make sure you send me pictures of that tree." Miss Peaches yelled out as they headed down the stairs.

"Oh, and Danielle….Thank you for everything." Lena yelled out after her mom, causing Dani to turn around and smile.

"No, thank you for everything." She yelled back, meaning it from the heart.

"We are all sisters now girl. We got each other's back." Lena assured her, making Danielle smile even harder.

Heading to pick up Mecca, Yana controlled the radio while Dani controlled the wheel. Pulling up in front of their condo, Dani snagged a parking spot and put the car in park. Snatching up her phone out of the cupholder, Danielle went to shoot Mecca a text but noticed Nike had sent her one instead.

Nike: Aye…. You know that warehouse across the street from the liquor store on Lake?

Dani: Yes

Nike: Meet me there NOW

Looking up from her phone and at the time on the dashboard, Danielle went to her contacts and called Mecca.

"Aye, I gotta bust a move real quick. I'm sending Yana upstairs. I'll be right back so we can go shopping." She said into the phone, ending the call before Mecca could object.

"I'll be back." She turned to Yana and said, hitting the locks so she could get out.

"I'll bring yo bag up when I come back. Call me when you get upstairs." Danielle told her, watching her until she no longer could.

Sitting in the same spot, Dani waited until she got that call from Yana before she headed towards the warehouse. With no clue in mind, she wondered what he wanted and why were they meeting there, out of all places? The drive there was less than five minutes, which is why she agreed so fast. Turning into the empty parking lot, she circled the lot until she found his car. Parking right next to him, Danielle texted Nike, letting him know she was outside before killing the engine. Hearing the phone chime, she unbuckled her seatbelt and just like she thought, he was telling her to come in. Doing as he requested, Dani headed towards the steel door when it opened up and out walked Nike.

"What we doing here?" she walked towards him and asked, looking around, checking her surroundings.

"Just come in. Come on." He said, pushing her forward and closing the door behind them.

The loud slam caused Dani to jump as Nike grabbed her hand, leading her deeper inside the dark warehouse. The only thing on her mind was, why were they there. The further they walked in, the colder it became, but Dani did notice a small amount of light ahead.

"Why are we here?" she whispered to him, squeezing his hand tighter.

"You'll see." Was all he said, just before they turned the corner.

Releasing her hand, Nike walked around the corner without saying a word, Danielle following behind him closely. Making it only a few feet, Dani stopped and froze at the sight in front of her.

"You know this nigga?" Nike walked over to her and asked, handing Danielle a black .22 Caliber gun.

Unable to speak or move, Danielle stood there stuck, staring at Dame, who was tied to a chair, slowly bleeding to death.

"IS THIS THE NIGGA THAT TOOK YOUR INNOCENCE? Nike yelled, pulling the gun back from Danielle and shooting Dame in the leg.

Dame's loud manly screams echoed through the warehouse, but it was no use, he couldn't be heard.

"Here, take this gun and pop this nigga." Nike urged, handing her the gun again, this time Dani took it.

Looking at Nike briefly, Danielle then focused her attention back on Dame as flashbacks of all the times he raped her, replayed in her head. It wasn't until she saw Yana, playing with the dolls, that it clicked. Dame was a nasty ass dog, and now that Danielle had to power to ensure he never raped another girl; she took advantage of it by placing two hot bullets inside his fucking skull.

Chapter Twenty-One

"Ms. Banks, you are all set. You can schedule your next appointment when you arrive in D.C. Here is your paperwork and best of luck to you and the baby on your new journey." Pip's favorite nurse's assistant Nicole said, coming around from behind the counter, giving Pip a hug.

"Thank you so much girl. I'll be sure to come by here whenever I visit." Pip lied as she walked out the door, staring at the ultrasound in her hand.

The December sun shined bright on Pip as she maneuvered through the snow to her car. Feeling the flutters in her stomach, Pip rubbed her belly as she thought about her future with her unborn child. It was crazy how you could love another human being so much, a little person that you haven't met yet. Pip felt like her daughter or son was what she's been missing the entire time.

Getting on the expressway at Halsted, Pip headed to her parent's house in Olympia Fields to speak with them before she left. Her flight was leaving that night, and just the thought of being in her new space sent warm chills through her body. Everything had worked out for the good, and although Pip thought she couldn't do it, she did it. The sound of her phone ringing snapped her out of her trance as she felt for it inside her purse. Almost swerving off the road twice, Pip finally was able to find it, answering it before the caller hung up.

"Hello Ms. Banks?" the caller queered from the other end as Pip placed the call on speaker.

"This is she." She replied, tapping the turning signal, switching lanes to exit.

"This is Mrs. Carol from Homestead Designs, just confirming that your home is done. I am emailing you over the final photos right now. I hope we fulfilled your dreams and that you love them. Please feel free to contact me with any questions or concerns."

After thanking her, Pip ended the call before stopping at the first red light and eagerly accessing the photos. Completely amazed by the first few pictures, Pip flipped through the rest and wanted to cry. Her home was indeed her dream home. Everything from the smallest details was just as she imagined in her head. The most beautiful part was the nursery. Although she didn't know what she was having, Pip decorated everything with neutral colors, and it turned out perfect.

Just as she turned onto her parent's block, her phone again, this time it was Nike calling.

"What's up bruh?" Pip answered, easing her way out of the car.

"I was just calling to say, I got that Mecca bitch too," Nike said, Pip automatically assuming that her ears were playing tricks on her.

"You lying Nike." She shockingly replied, slamming the car door shut.

"Nah, I got the bitch coming outta the store. Put her ass in the trunk. Slit her throat. Now she somewhere swimming with the fishes." Nike explained in detail, his words were like music to her ears.

"Thanks a lot. That drop will be in yo account in five minutes. I'll holler at you later." Pip said, ending the call as she happily walked into her parent's house.

With both of them being gone, Pip could sleep a little better at night and although Capone was still alive and well, she knew his day was coming soon.

"Hey, mom. Hey dad!" Pip yelled through the house as she searched for her parents.

Hearing noise coming from downstairs in the basement, Pip headed down there but to only find the noise coming from the tv. Turning around, heading back up the stairs, Pip slipped and fell on what she assumed was snow. Breaking her fall with her wrist, she slowly got up when she noticed the palm of her hands were wet. Looking down, she almost had a heart attack, as blood covered both of her hands.

Hesitantly turning her head to the right, Pip screamed at the sight of both of her parents laying in a puddle of blood. Shaking uncontrollably, she tried to think of the best thing to do, but she came up empty. Scared as shit, Pip wiped her hands off on a shirt that was laying on the couch and ran up the stairs.

Running through the kitchen and passed the front door, she headed up the stairs that led to the bedroom, making a sharp left into her parent's room. Rushing to the walk-in closet, Pip pushed back all the clothes, revealing a silver and black safe. Quickly entering the code and getting it right on the first try. Pip grabbed all the cash that was inside, which was well over two-thousand, and stuffed it in her bag. Turning and running away quickly, Pip headed to the airport, no doubt being early for her flight.

Her parents and their lives were never part of the plan, it was just one of the casualties. Most daughters or even human beings for that matter would have at least called the police but not Pip. Pip knew they would do nothing but slow her down.

Remembering about the few more thousands in cash that her parents kept behind the tv in the den. Pip made a pit stop there and grabbed those coins too before really dashing out the house. Smiling to herself as she thought about her getaway, Pip began to map out her new life with her new baby and new baby daddy. With all the money she was running away with, she could hire ten hitmen to kill Capone and whoever else. Feeling like the Griselda Blanco of the pimp game, Pip stepped out of her parent's house without ever looking back. Heading to the car with her purse full of money, Pip looked down the street where she noticed police flying up the block with their sirens blaring.

The first car stopping at the very end of the street while the others filed in, eventually blocking off the entire block. Cops jumped out in full action; their guns raised high, ready to shoot at any minute. The cops stayed at their vehicles, while two white men in suits and trench coats walked across the street towards her.

"Ava Banks." He spoke, raising his badge high in the air so the whole neighborhood could see it.

"You are under arrest for the killing of Coby Young and MacArthur Smith…"

"What? Coby Young? MacArthur Smith? I think there's been a mix up somewhere." She pleaded as they forcefully placed her hands behind her back.

Everything from that point on moved in slow motion. Turns out, Capone was able to get those tapes pulled from the day Pip hit Coby. Seeing that it was a deadly hit and run, they were eager to bring her in. As far as Mac's murder, Capone had Mac's body placed in the trunk of one of her cars. The night that Brandy came over, she slipped something into Pip's wine, knocking her out cold. Grabbing her phone, she sent a text message from Pip's phone to Mac's phone, pretty much incriminating herself, pointing the fingers even more towards her. Although life in jail was nothing like spending eternity in hell, Pip was right where everybody needed her to be.

Epilogue

Two Years Later

"Yana sit down and do yo homework…. And please get yo knees off my couch."

"MECCA WOULD YOU COME GET HER AND TAKE HER HOME!" Dani yelled at the top of her lungs as she marched to the back of the house were Mecca was located.

"Girl, what you fussing about now?" Mecca asked, looking up from her laptop at her younger sister.

"Yana won't listen. She supposed to be doing her homework at the kitchen table, yet she on the couch on her phone." Danielle snitched from the spot she was standing at by the door while Mecca got off the bed.

Walking through the huge penthouse apartment on the seventh floor, Danielle looked around at her home and smiled. She had come a long way from roaches and holes in the wall.

"Yana put yo shoes on. Capone should be pulling up any minute now. "Mecca said, heading over to the couch herself.

"I'm stopping by the beauty supply first thing in the morning after I drop Yana off at school. Then I'll meet up with you after I leave the bank." Mecca advised her as she tied up her Gucci shoes.

Snatching up Yana's Burberry raincoat, Dani handed it to her as she walked past.

"Damn you putting us out?" Mecca snapped, twisting her head in Danielle's direction.

"I bet Nike coming over." Yana chimed in as she put her bookbag on her back.

"STAY IN A CHILD'S PLACE!" Both Danielle and Mecca said in unison as Yana smacked her lips.

"But to answer your questions, yes, I am putting you out, and yes, it is because of Nike. My man has been out of town for almost and week, and now that he's back, I'm about to back it up!" Danielle said, sticking her tongue out as she playfully twerked on Mecca.

"Ummmm language around my child," Mecca warned her, covering up Yana's ear with her hands.

Since having full custody of Yana, Mecca was in complete parent mode, all the time. Although she was only twenty-one, Mecca acted like an old granny, especially when it came to protecting Yana. Everything she did revolved around that little girl, but Dani wouldn't have it any other way.

"How are Brandy and Cameron?" Mecca asked out of the blue as she continued to get Yana ready.

"They are good. I'm going to get him tomorrow and taking him to the zoo." Dani said, smiling at the thought of her Godson.

Danielle had been in love with Brandy's baby, Cameron, from the moment she laid eyes on him in the hospital. After Brandy asked if she would be his Godmother, Danielle accepted it with honor. Doing whatever she had to do, Brandy lied to Pip and told her that she got an abortion, just to get in closer with her.

"Speaking of God kids, how are Ashlee and Conor?" Danielle asked her just as Yana began to tug at her arm.

"They good. I'm going over there the first chance I get." Mecca answered her, swatting away at Yana.

"And what about Stephany? Is she still in Puerto Rico?"

Walking over to the front door to see who was on the bell, Danielle looked at the camera and noticed that not only was Nike standing there but so was Capone.

"They must have pulled up together," Dani mumbled to herself before buzzing them in.

After altering all of Pip's bank documents, Steph took Dani up on her offer and moved to Puerto Rico, all-expenses paid on behalf of Danielle Young. When Pip got booked for the murder of Coby and Mac, all of her paperwork had Danielle's name on them as Power of Attorney. Seeing how she was behind bars and incapable of handling her own estate, everything belonged to Danielle. Pip thinking that she was smarter than your average bear, pleaded insanity which deemed Danielle the sole owner of every single thing in her name.

Opening the front door for the guys, Danielle greeted Nike with the biggest hug while Capone and Mecca kissed.

"What's up baby? What's up Mecca? Where Yana at?" Nike soke, his hands still palming Danielle's ass.

"What up Nike. Her ass in the back somewhere on that phone. How was Atlanta?" Mecca asked him as Capone headed to the back to check on Yana.

Nike filled the ladies in on his business trip just as Capone returned from the back by himself.

"She's knocked out. She might as well stay the night here. Come on baby." Capone said, ushering Mecca towards the door.

"No the hell yall not. She cannot stay here. Go get yall child." Dani yelled loud enough to wake her and the whole building up.

Feeling her phone vibrate in her pocket, she pulled it out, reading the message from Troy.

Troy: BITCH TURN ON THE NEWS NOW! CHANNEL NINE!

Outside of gaining a dope friendship with Brandy, Danielle found a friend in Troy as well. Keeping her promise like she said would, Dani paid for Troy's Grandmother's house and handed the keys over to her. With help from Brandy, the two of them ran what used to Pip's House but is currently known as Coby's World.

"Where the remote? Who seen the remote?" Danielle panicked, looking around the living room while everyone looked at her crazy.

Turning to the channel nine news, Danielle turned the tv up as soon as she saw Pip's face on the big screen.

"The trial of Ava Banks was set to start next week for the murder of Coby Young and MacArthur Smith. Cook County sheriffs made a chilling discovery today when they found Ms. Bank, hanging in her cell. Turns out, another inmate by the name of Melissa Young, beat, stabbed and cut off Ms. Banks fingers before hanging her to her death. As the story unfolds, Ms. Banks was serving time for the murder of Ms. Young's son. When word got back about the two women sharing a jail cell, Ms. Young killed Ms. Banks. More on this story at ten. Back to you in the studio Liu Yung."

Turning the tv off, no one in the room showed the less bit of concern or care regarding the news segment they had seen. Truthfully, no one spoke about Pip since then, it was like she vanished out of all their lives the day she went to jail. With Capone getting rid of her parents, legally, it all belonged to Danielle with assistance from Miss Peaches' daughter, Lena.

After turning over the proof she needed to catch her husband cheating with one of Pip's girls. Lena pulled BIG strings, getting Pip's name legally removed from everything. Judge Lena promised Danielle and Mecca that there would be no trace of Pip when she was done. Leaving all of Pip's bank accounts, those in the states and across seas in their name. Leaving all her property, including stocks and bonds in their name as well. The Young Sisters were on their way to becoming millionaires before they turned twenty-five. Showing you the true meaning of FROM RATCHET TO RICHE$

THE END!!